A Trip Back in Time

A Novel by,

EDWIN F. BECKER

AuthorHouse™
1663 Liberty Drive
Bloomington, IN 47403
www.authorhouse.com
Phone: 1-800-839-8640

This is a complete work of fiction. All of the characters, names, incidents, organizations, and dialogue in this novel are either the products of the author's imagination or are used fictionally.

First published by AuthorHouse 6/13/2011

ISBN: 978-1-4567-6279-7 (e)
ISBN: 978-1-4567-6280-3 (dj)
ISBN: 978-1-4567-6281-0 (sc)

Library of Congress Control Number: 2011906316

Printed in the United States of America

Other Books By, Edwin F. Becker

Banished
A Demon, an Exorcist and a battle of faith

The Eleventh Commandment
Let he who harms the children be struck down

DeathWalker
A Vampire's Vengeance

Visit Ed at
www.edwinbecker.com

This is dedicated to my Granddaughters;
LeeAnn, Krystal, Ashlee and Madeline…
And to my children, who gave me these gifts.

Chapter One

THEY SAT ON THE PATIO facing the fourth hole in a plush, gated golf community. It was a sunny morning, and it was also LeeAnn's birthday. She chose to spend the whole weekend with her grandparents. She loved talking with her Papa because he seemed to know everything. However (and even better) when he didn't, he would just make up all kinds of funny stuff.

"**When I was your age,** they didn't have houses built on golf courses like this." LeeAnn's grandfather explained.

"Papa, why don't you get a golf cart?" She asked, as a parade of golf carts drove alongside his property.

He smiled. "Well, for a starter, I don't golf."

"But Papa, we could drive it around and have fun." The '*we*' she was referring to was her younger sister, Ashlee, and her two cousins, Krystal and Madeline. They normally attended their grandparent's home together, but this was LeeAnn's birthday weekend and she was enjoying having her grandparents to herself. Her sister and cousins would arrive later in the day. LeeAnn was ten years old today, but far more mature and perceptive than your average ten year old. She was entering the age of '*tween*', as it is referred to. This is the uncomfortable age of no longer being a child, but not yet an adolescent. She had blonde hair with bright blue eyes, that sparkled as she kidded with her Papa.

"Come on, Papa, buy a golf cart. It would be a blast!"

"When I was your age, we didn't have golf carts." He answered.

LeeAnn gazed out at the vast acreage of what was only two of eighteen fairways in sight, and gasped.

"Are you telling me that they carried those heavy golf bags for the whole game?"

"No. Some had wheels on the bags, so you could pull them along, but mostly they had caddies. Caddies were typically high school kids that would carry the bags for the golfer and make a few bucks."

"Papa, I wouldn't carry the bags for a hundred dollars all that way." She replied.

"**When I was your age,** that's what they did and they were happy to do it to make a little money."

"Come on Papa. Are you sure you didn't have dinosaurs pulling golf wagons?" She laughed.

"Okay, I realize it sounds a bit absurd, but that is how it was and we loved every minute of those years. I never realized that the *'Good old days'* were really the good old days!"

Papa laughed and pointed. "Just look at that guy with headphones on. If someone yells 'fore,' he is not going to hear them and will likely get hit in the head by a golf ball. Must everyone today have something stuffed in their ears?"

"Oh, Papa, you slay me!" She laughed.

"LeeAnn, learn to spot an idiot when you see one. He probably comes from a long line of idiots that were sent here from Europe. A little known fact is that in 1492, Columbus really arrived with four ships, not three. There was the Nina, the Pinta, the Santa Maria…and then this last ship, the Idiota. It was this last ship that was filled with idiots that Europe sent to Spain to get rid of. No one ever talks about that fourth ship, but those idiots spread out all over America. Come to think of it, maybe getting a good shot in the head with a golf ball will straighten out his whole gene pool!"

LeeAnn just laughed, as Papa always seemed to make fun of everything current. Just then, the patio door opened and her Nana announced "Breakfast is ready! Come in before it gets cold."

LeeAnn surveyed the table, which was filled with pancakes, a platter of scrambled eggs, a pile of bacon, and stack of toast. "Geez Nana, this is what I call breakfast."

"What do you normally eat, young lady?" Nana asked.

"Oh, a pop tart, or maybe just some cereal."

"**When I was your age,** this is what we normally ate in the morning. We could never face the day without a good, hearty breakfast."

"Nana, did they really carry those heavy golf bags in the old days, or was Papa just making up one of his stories?"

"They sure did. Even the women golfers carried their own clubs, but most used caddies. Did he explain what caddies were?"

"Yeah, but I thought he was just kidding. What's a fore?" She asked.

"Fore means to be forewarned, and is what a golfer yells when he hits the ball where people might be in the general vicinity. It warns them to watch out." She explained.

"Papa called a guy wearing an iPod an idiot!" she laughed.

"Well if he can't hear what is going on around him, a golf course is not the best place to be walking around. I would say your grandfather is right. He pretty much knows an idiot when he sees one."

LeeAnn piled her plate, as this breakfast was a real treat. Meanwhile, Papa did his usual mock-complaining.

"Where's the sausage and French toast? Woman, what are you, on vacation?" He growled.

"Old man, you are lucky to get that. With your heart, I should pile your plate with tofu." Nana snapped back.

LeeAnn just laughed, as this is how Nana and Papa normally kidded one another. Forty-four years of marriage had bonded them, and their love for one another radiated--regardless of their verbal jousting. Just watching them was humorous, as Papa was six foot three and Nana was barely five feet tall, yet she bossed him around and he knew never to push her limits.

"Nana, this is great!" LeeAnn complemented.

"Well, it's really nothing dear. **When I was your age** we would also have some sliced tomatoes to go with those eggs and a bowl of fruit."

The relationship between grandparents and grandchildren can be unique and special. From a grandchild's perspective, at first they don't know exactly where grandparents fit within the family order. They initially know they smile and like them, but it's only later that they understand that their parents were once their grandparent's children, and as grandchildren they will always receive unconditional love and acceptance that is unmatched in life. All too soon they become used to being showered with lots of good things in concentrated doses.

No sooner than breakfast was over, LeeAnn gathered the plates and cleared the table, proceeding in helping her Nana in the kitchen.

"Thank you, dear." Nana said as she went about her business cleaning the kitchen. "The only time your grandfather will help with the dishes is when we have takeout food! He throws the bags away and then boldly announces 'I did the dishes today!' He is really something!"

As if offended, Papa yelled from the living room. "Are you talking about me?"

"You quiet down or I'll really hurt you!" Nana shouted back.

Meanwhile LeeAnn giggled loudly. "Nana, you and Papa are funny! When Papa tells me about when he was a child, is he kidding?"

"No, likely not. You know when he is kidding, because it will really be a whopper. No, **when we were your age** things were a lot different. You see all the stuff in our freezer? 90% of it did not exist. Frozen dinners were brand new and nobody had a refrigerator this size. I could never imagine getting water or ice right from the door. In fact, even the word microwave did not exist. Everything happened on the stove."

"Cooking was that different?" LeeAnn asked.

"Oh yes! Almost everything was made from scratch. We even made our own biscuits. We did have canned vegetables, but we had very few prepared meats. You had to go to a butcher shop or the delicatessen for cold cuts. Way back then, I could never imagine a store like Wal-Mart, where you could get almost everything under one roof. We went from store to store. Papa and I grew up in very different environments, as I grew up in a small town in Texas and Papa grew up in the center of Chicago, which is a huge city."

"How did you get to Missouri?" LeeAnn asked.

"Well, Papa just decided it was better for us all, once he was done working. Someday maybe we will sit down and I will explain the whole story, but Papa and I always loved Branson. We were first here in 1967 and fell in love with these beautiful mountains."

"Did you help your mom when you were young?" LeeAnn questioned.

"**When I was your age**, I did an awful lot. But we didn't have the things we have today."

LeeAnn was curious. "Like what?"

"We had no vacuum cleaners, for one. We had a carpet sweeper. Plus, floors had none of these protective coatings; we had to scrub and wax. Yes, cleaning was different...in a bad way." She laughed. "We used a lot of kitchen cleanser, which was an abrasive powder."

Just then, the doorbell rang and Ashlee, Krystal and Madeline came running in. They went straight to Nana with hugs and kisses, but as usual they all immediately asked "Where's Papa?"

"Where's my girls?" Papa bellowed from the front room.

"Can we stay the night?" The three asked at once.

"You must get permission from your parents, but this day belongs to LeeAnn." Papa responded as little Madeline jumped in his lap.

"We want one of your stories!" Ashlee demanded.

LeeAnn was smiling smugly. "Nana was telling me how we came to live in Missouri." She bragged.

"Tell us Papa!" They demanded.

They could tell by the expression on his face that everything he was about to say was one of his wild, fabricated tales.

"Well, it was back in 1998 that we loaded all our stuff in the wagons and pointed the horses west. It was a dangerous time, as the west was wild with Indians. I don't know which was more dangerous, fighting the great Indian war of 1999, or having to swim across the mighty Mississippi!" He was grinning the whole time.

"Well, if you swam across, how did Nana get across?" Ashlee wisely asked.

"Ah, I put Nana on my back. I even put Benjii on my back!"

Benjii the Shih Tzu wagged his tail as if he knew Papa was telling a tall story.

Krystal looked at him in wonder and asked "Papa, are you telling the truth?"

"This I swear; everything I just said was all a bunch of bull plop!" He laughed.

"Papa, told me a bunch of stuff about when he **when he was our age,** for real!" LeeAnn bragged.

"Tell us Papa! Come on!"

He looked at the innocent faces and wondered if they would ever realize how much this world has changed in the fifty plus years that divided them. The times were certainly different, and his culture had been as innocent as their little faces. But, he decided to throw out a few tidbits. As soon as he began, he knew this curious group would not let him rest.

"**When I was your age**, we had no computers at all. We didn't even have calculators!" he stated.

LeeAnn chuckled. "What did you do, Papa, use your fingers and toes?"

Her younger sister Ashlee thought this was hysterical and began laughing, as did her cousins, Krystal and Madeline.

Krystal laughed. "Papa had to count on his toes!"

"I suppose they still had horses." Ashlee joked.

Papa smiled. "As a matter of fact, they did. Horse drawn wagons would come down the alley and a junk man would collect whatever things he thought were valuable from the garbage. Plus, a horse drawn vegetable wagon would also use the alley and the vendor would yell out

'POTATOOOOES! TOMATOOOOES!' and he would ring a bell. He would yell so loud you could hear him for a block. Then the housewives would rush out and buy fresh produce."

Leave it to Ashlee to ask "Who cleaned up the horse poop?"

All the girls laughed. This made Papa scratch his head.

"You know, I don't really know?"

LeeAnn was giggling hysterically. Her blue eyes were starting to tear up.

Krystal was confused. "What's an alley?"

"Well, in the city they had something like a street that was behind the houses by our garages. Our garages were in the back of the house, along with garbage cans."

As usual, it was Ashlee that asked "Did you ever step in the horse poop?"

"No, but I had a few friends that did!"

"Papa, my face hurts from laughing! Now tell us how far you walked to school." Krystal wondered.

"Well, since my mother and father were divorced and I lived with both of them at various times, it was not unusual to walk eight city blocks, which is about a mile. It was a lot different living in the city of Chicago, than where you live now, in Nixa, Missouri. How far do you walk?"

LeeAnn answered first. "We walk to the corner and the bus picks us up. We have buses now, Papa!"

All the girls were cracking up.

"Oh you mean you don't have your own cars yet?" He joked. "You tell your parents that I expect all of you to get your own cell phones and credit cards. You poor babies are living in poverty."

"I have my own cell phone already." LeeAnn bragged.

"Who do you call?" Papa asked.

"I mostly text." She answered.

"You know phones were invented so people could actually talk to each other."

"Yeah, but I can text in school and communicate when I can't talk." She quickly replied.

"Well, **when I was your age**, we had what was called '*party lines,*' where more than one family shared a phone number."

"Get out! How can you share a cell phone?" LeeAnn asked.

"Oh, it was easy, because there were no cell phones. There were only land lines. You picked up the phone and if another family was having a conversation, you hung up until they were done." Papa explained.

"No cell phones?" They all gasped.

"Did you ever listen in and hear other people talking?" Krystal questioned.

"Oh, all the time. When I was younger, I thought it was funny to pick up the phone and make a farting noise!"

Now he had them all laughing hysterically. Even the youngest, Madeline, was laughing, as they all started mimicking conversations interrupted by farting noises. LeeAnn, the oldest, was sharp as could be and just could not believe there were such times.

"Come on Papa, are you telling us the truth?"

"I swear. That's how it was."

In the front room was a projection television that displayed a 120 inch picture. Papa pointed to it. "You see that monster of a TV? **When I was your age,** our televisions were only this big." He made about a 15 inch gap between his hands. "And, there was no color, only black and white."

"Get out!" Ashlee replied.

"I wish I could go back in time and see this for myself..." LeeAnn replied.

"Let me tell you about Winky Dink, and how he got all the kids in trouble."

They all laughed.

"What the heck is a Winky Dink?" Ashlee asked.

"Well, Winky Dink was one of the early cartoon characters, like Dora the Explorer, or Sponge Bob. His show was on Saturday mornings on black and white TV. The stores sold a Winky Dink set that everyone was expected to buy, but hardly anybody did. It was a clear plastic cover that you were supposed to put over your TV screen. When Winky Dink came on, the bad guys would chase Winky Dink and he would have to escape by trying to cross a cliff that was too far to jump. The announcer would then tell the kids to draw a line on the TV that would represent a bridge, and a few seconds later Winky Dink would run across. This made it appear like the kids saved him. Then he would say to draw some stairs Winky Dink could climb, which they did, etc. The television got really messed up, because kids drew with crayons all over them, since nobody bought the Winky Dink set with the plastic cover. Kids all over the nation were drawing with crayons on the television screen. Parents became angry, kids were getting punished, and Winky Dink was quickly over and taken off TV."

Ashlee just laughed at the name. "Winky Dink?" she giggled.

"I can't imagine kids drawing with crayons on the television. Man, their parents had to be mad. I would never do that." LeeAnn replied.

"Oh, the guy on television actually encouraged them to do it! Even I didn't understand why my dad was spanking me, when all I did was save Winky Dink!"

"Gee Papa, I wish I could have seen all this. It sounds so funny. I wish we could go back in time." LeeAnn said smiling.

"Well, maybe that should be your birthday wish. Tonight, when you blow out the candles, make a wish. You never know. It just might come true." Papa suggested.

Yes, LeeAnn seemed to enjoy knowing what her Papa had experienced and as they talked and laughed, he made a wish that she really could see what it was like.

That evening, the whole family gathered to sing Happy Birthday to LeeAnn. Afterward, she concentrated really hard and made her wish. She wished she could see the world that her Papa had grown up in. As the candles were blown out, she felt a strange tingling feeling, but thought it was because she had blown so hard that she was out of breath. The opening of the presents was always fun and the evening seemed to zip right by. Everyone eventually went home, leaving LeeAnn to spend the last night of her birthday weekend with her grandparents. It had been a long and fun filled day, and she anxiously tucked herself into the king size bed in their guest room. Her thoughts were filled with the discussions about the old days. *'Life without cell phones? Weird.'* This was her last thought, before falling into a deep sleep.

Was Papa a wizard? Or did her wish come true? But she swears to this day that the next morning, she woke up in Chicago and it was 1956!

It was a shock when LeeAnn awoke to the brash sound of a Big Ben windup alarm clock. As she looked about the room, everything had changed. She immediately noticed the walls had wallpaper of some antique floral design. She noticed her headboard was cast iron instead of wood, and in place of a down quilt, she was covered in what looked to be some type of homemade bedspread. In the center of the ceiling was a plain light fixture, rather than her pretty chandelier. Other than the brash sounding clock, the top of the nightstand was empty. Her diary was gone, along with her cell phone. Then, she heard a car horn and went to the open window. She was confused, as she looked out and realized she was on the second floor of a building facing a very busy city street! The cars were like she had never seen before but in movies, and yet all appeared brand new? There were cables hanging above the street and as she watched in amazement, a bus went by with a rod on the back attached to the cables. As it passed, she watched the sparks fly where the rod and cable met, making a crackling sound. She then looked down at her pajamas, realizing they were plain flannel. '*What is happening*?' She wondered. She then screamed "Mom!"

When her mother walked into the room, LeeAnn's jaw dropped, as her mom had on a long house dress and her hair was lying flat with an upward curl at the tip, just above her shoulders. Her mom had very little make-up on, and no eye shadow? '*Is this a dream or a nightmare?'* She wondered.

"Get ready for school young lady!" Mom ordered. "Today is the last day! Tomorrow you can sleep in, if you like. Even though it's a half day, I made you a lunch."

'*Made me a lunch?'* LeeAnn was baffled. "Mom, I'll eat at school."

"Eat what? They only serve milk in the lunch room?" Her mother gave her a confused look.

"No, the cafeteria." LeeAnn snapped back.

"What are you talking about? There is no cafeteria! Are you completely awake yet?"

LeeAnn was now very confused. She knew this was not her world. She pinched herself, finding that neither was this a dream. She went into the bathroom, and stared in awe. The fixtures looked older than anything she had ever seen. There was no vanity, just a white sink bolted to the wall. On the sink was a cup with toothbrushes in it, and even they looked antique. On a nearby shelf sat all of her mom's cosmetics, which were few. She did see hair spray, but no hand held hair dryer in sight. There was not even an electrical outlet anywhere near the mirror, which was actually an old medicine cabinet. She opened the medicine cabinet, and there sat a tube of toothpaste labeled IPANA. Next to it was something labeled tooth powder, and some Bayer aspirin. She found herself staring at a number of strange products. '*Castor oil? Witch Hazel? Cold Cream? Iodine? Weird.'* She then realized that there was no shower curtain. In fact, there was no shower, only a bath tub. LeeAnn quickly determined that the smaller toothbrush was hers, and brushed her teeth. She did not want a bath, and all she could find was a huge white bar of soap. So she washed her face and returned to her room to choose her clothes. When she opened the door, again came a shock. There were a number of long dresses, some pants that appeared tight at the ankle, and some jeans. She tried on the jeans, and they were too long, so she rolled them up. Searching for a top, she could only find long sleeve blouses and sweaters.

Looking around for anything that resembled shoes, she could only find two pair, which were real leather. One pair was very shiny, and she had never seen patent leather before. She made the assumption that these must be 'dress' shoes because they were so shiny. The second pair were what was called 'penny loafers', and indeed had pennies tucked into the tops. In her tiny dresser, she found nothing but white socks. As she put them on, she instinctively folded them over, and then slid on the loafers, which felt stiff and uncomfortable. *'No wonder they invented Nikes.'* She thought. Still in a bit of confusion and feeling like she was wearing someone else's clothes, she proceeded to the kitchen for breakfast.

As she entered the kitchen, her mom scowled.

"Young lady, you know jeans are not allowed at school. Go put on one of your school dresses."

LeeAnn returned to her room and looked at the few dresses. She quickly realized that three were identical, and must be a uniform of some kind. *'These are embarrassing…'* she thought, but picked one out and put it on. It hung almost down to her ankles. Suddenly she looked around and wondered *'Where is my sister Ashlee?'* She began examining everything in the room. The first thing she noticed was that all of her stuff was gone. There was no M3P player, and her Nintendo DS was gone. Her work books were sitting on a chair, and she did not see her backpack? She sat on her bed and knew better than to even look for her cell phone. She pondered '*What year is this*?' She grabbed the brush off the top of her dresser and began brushing her hair. She looked into the mirror. "What will I do with this hair? No shower, no gel, no conditioner?" She whispered. It was then that her mom walked in and without a word, grabbed her hair and pulled it back. With a quick flick of the wrist and a rubber band, she made an instant pony tail.

"Breakfast, young lady." She ordered.

"I'll just have a Pop Tart."

"A what?" Her mom asked.

"A Pop Tart?" LeeAnn answered, with less certainty in her voice.

"What in the world is a pop tart?" Her mom asked, emphasizing both the words 'pop' and 'tart'.

"Ah, never mind. What am I having?"

"Cornflakes, of course. You know I have to get to work today."

LeeAnn knew better than to say anything else, as it seemed she knew little of this world she was in. *'Is this a dream, or did I get my wish? Is this 1956?'* She wondered. The kitchen really looked old, as the refrigerator was tiny. There was only a small counter top. Beside the toaster sat a gigantic mixer. There was no electric can opener, nor was there a microwave. There was a box-type thing on the counter, which she got up and promptly opened it. All it contained was bread. *'A box for bread? Weird.'* She sat at the table, and in front of her bowl of cornflakes was huge bowl of sugar. She sprinkled it on and as she stirred up the bowl, she spilt some of the milk on the table. She instantly got up and quickly realized there were no paper towels. So instead, she wiped it up with a washrag that was on the sink. As she ate, she noticed a broom leaning against the wall in the corner. *'This is really strange.'* She thought to herself, shaking her head. Only after she was finished did she realize there was no dishwasher! *'This is just not real. It must be a dream!'*

She opened the refrigerator, and the inside was tiny. There were no shelves inside the door, and the milk was in a huge glass jug. She stared at a few strange items. *'What is Crisco?'* She wondered, as she looked at what appeared to be a coffee-type can which read 'shortening.' *'What is Milnot?'* She picked up the can and it read concentrated milk. *'Where are the Lunchables?'*

Her mom entered and handed her a square metal lunch box. She looked at it, and it was decorated with children's characters. *'Come on, Tinker Bell?'* She started to feel like a real dork. She was anxious to get out and into the street, but had no idea what school she was going to and where to catch the school bus?

"Don't forget your workbooks, young lady!" Her mom yelled.

She walked through the apartment, observing everything on her way. It was all so plain and sparse. She noticed that there was a telephone, but it looked huge! It was black, and a coil cord was attached to the receiver. *'I wonder if that is a party line, like Papa said?'* She opened the front door, and walked down the stairs. As she walked out the door, she realized that they were living above a store. The sign above it read "Waluska's Delicatessen." *'I heard Nana use that word. What the heck is a delicatessen?'* She turned around and saw a boy about her age watching her and smiling. He was about her height, but was very skinny. He had blond hair and piercing brown eyes that had a bit of a twinkle. Somehow, his eyes and smile seemed distantly familiar.

"LeeAnn!" He called.

"You know me?"

"Yeah! And you know me." He answered, smiling.

"Who are you?" She asked.

"It's me, Papa!" He laughed.

"Papa?" She gasped. "Are you crazy? Do you know who Papa is?"

"Yes, LeeAnn, I'm your grandfather. You wanted to know what kind of world I grew up in, so I decided to give you the tour. Welcome to 1956."

"Get out!"

"No, this is for real." He laughed.

"If you're my Papa, then tell me something only Papa would know." She asked.

He smiled knowingly. "Well, where do I start? You love root beer and your favorite color is orange. You seem to enjoy the letters I write you. Most times, I send you money to distribute to your sister and your cousins. I know their names. Krystal, Madeline, and your sister, Ashlee."

"Papa, you are so small!" As they talked, she walked totally around him, examining him from head to toe.

"Well, we are both the same age! It is 1956 and I could only take you back to the time when I was your exact age. You shouldn't call me Papa in public. Call me Ed." He knew she would be filled with wonder, and had created a few pleasant surprises. LeeAnn's mom and dad were actually divorced, but for this journey, Papa had put them together.

"Papa where are we?"

"This is Chicago. We are where it is called the near north side."

"Papa, where is everything?"

"Remember…I'm Ed. By everything, I assume you mean technology, like cell phones and whatnot. Well, I hate to tell you this, but none of that has been invented yet."

"Mom looked so different."

"Yeah, I bet. She is working part-time, and your dad will be home after work."

"Mom and dad are together? Where's Ashlee?"

"Well I thought seeing your mom and dad together might make you happy. In fact, if they really were in 1956, I doubt whether they would have ever divorced. This may look like a backward time, but it was much kinder, and the future always held such promise. As far as Ashlee, she will take her own journey in a few years. Right now it is you and I, and the year is 1956."

"No Nana?"

"Nope! Right now your Nana is only eight years old and likely in San Marcos, Texas. It's a wonder that we ever met, when you think about it."

LeeAnn smiled. "Will anything we do affect history? Like in that old movie, Back to the Future?"

Papa chuckled. "No! Not to worry. Nothing you can do will change anything. The only thing is that I must experience this journey exactly as it was. I must experience the major things that effected my childhood. Some of it is good, and some of it is bad, but that is my price for bringing you here." Papa grinned. "How do you like the cool lunch box?"

"I feel like a dork. Where are the back packs?"

"They haven't been invented yet." Papa laughed. "You'll be hearing that a lot from me while we are here. So, what's for lunch?"

"PB&J, I think."

"Don't say 'PB&J', as no one will understand. No one uses acronyms yet."

LeeAnn fixed her stare on him.

"What?" He asked.

"Papa…Ed, you look so small!"

"Funny, isn't it? I was small. I really didn't grow much until I was in high school. Don't say it--my hair is really this blonde and yes, I am pretty skinny."

"Are you hungry?" LeeAnn asked in a concerned way.

"Nah, I eat pretty good. Even when I am on my own, in 1956, it is easy to get food. Here, follow me."

They walked a few stores down and encountered the greatest smell, billowing into the street. It was an old fashioned bakery. LeeAnn had never seen a store that only sold baked goods, and the variety of cakes, sweet rolls and breads she found incredible. They looked inside, and there were three older women dressed in white aprons scurrying around the counter as a few people holding cards with numbers on them stood around.

"Watch this."

Papa walked in and boldly went to the counter. A smiling old woman asked "How can I help you honey?"

With a sad expression, Papa said "I am so hungry, and I don't have any money. Can I get a donut please?"

The old woman smiled. "Wait one second." She walked over and got a small white paper bag. In it, she placed a chocolate donut and added a few cookies. "Here sweetie."

As he smiled broadly and accepted the bag, Papa replied "Thank you very much!"

She smiled back. "Honey, if you are ever hungry, you come here and let me know."

After leaving the store, Papa showed LeeAnn what was in the bag. "Here, try some."

"Papa…er...Ed…these are delicious!"

"Well, it is the pure, real ingredients. Not like what you are used to. In fact, maybe that is why I am so small, as the food has no additives and no preservatives. This is what butter, sugar, flour, and yeast really taste like if they are mixed right! What you witnessed is not unusual. At my age, I can go almost anywhere and just ask, and I'll get a handout…or should I say, sample. Well, that is as long as I don't wear out my welcome."

"Papa, er…Ed, this whole world is like a giant museum." LeeAnn just gazed at the cars going by and stated "They look so huge."

"They are! You will see names that you are unfamiliar with, like Hudson, Desoto, or Packard. What you won't see, is any foreign cars, except maybe a rare VW. Japan is not making cars yet; in fact, at this point in history, Japan is known for tin toys and cheap ceramics. Today, something that states 'made in Japan' is not a great thing. If you have a television, it will likely be an Admiral, Zenith, Motorola, or maybe even a Muntz. Everything is made in America."

"What do mean 'if' we have a TV?" She asked in surprise.

"Well televisions are becoming common, but not everyone can afford one. Oh yeah, they are also all black and white. Plus, there are only three channels."

"No cable?"

"Nope!"

"No Nickelodeon?"

"Nope."

"No color?"

"Nope. Right now, my mom and dad are separated. I live with my dad and although I like it because he just leaves me on my own for days, when I go home, there is no TV, or even a radio."

"Oh my God! What do you do?"

"Well, if I have nothing to do and go home early, I read."

"Am I going to school today?"

"Yes. In fact, we better get a move on. This is the last day before summer vacation and we only have a half day."

"Ed, but I am already on summer vacation?" LeeAnn replied.

"Sorry, but in 1956, we went to school until nearly the end of June."

"What school am I going to?"

"Saint Philomena's. I will give you a taste of what a Catholic school was once like."

LeeAnn noticed Ed was wearing plain blue pants and a short sleeve white shirt. As they walked, she watched as he produced a clip on tie from his pocket and put it on. She could not help but stare at him, because although she knew it was her Papa, the image of this skinny boy was strange. She knew he was only ten, but he walked with a swagger and confidence that was foreign to the boys of her age group. She followed along and could not help but notice that there was no store that looked anywhere near familiar. They were all little store fronts that were specialized, as she could tell from the signs. Some of them amazed her, like the shoe shop, where it appeared they only repaired shoes. She already saw a bakery, but now they passed a butcher shop that only sold meat and had a cage of live chickens. As they walked, she saw a tailor, a photographer, and then she asked "What is a grill?"

"A grill is like our fast food place. It isn't quite a restaurant, and only serves food that can be made quickly like hamburgers, eggs, various sandwiches etc. Most are open 24 hours." Ed explained.

"What about McDonald's?"

"Nope."

"Chucky Cheese?"

"Nope."

"Baskin's?"

"Nope."

"Domino's?"

"All not here yet. In fact, as you know it, there is no fast food. Our version is a grill, or a hot dog stand."

"Papa...Ed, this sucks!"

"Nah, it's not so bad. You'll see."

As they reached the corner, there was a store that displayed a confectionary sign. Out front was a steel table with newspapers piled high, and coins lying out in the open. "What is that?" She questioned.

"A confectionary is like a neighborhood 'Quick Stop' type store. Every neighborhood has one or two. They have bread, milk, eggs and food staples, plus candy, cigarettes, comics, magazines and, as you can see, newspapers. Newspapers are important as far as getting information. Chicago actually has four; the Tribune, the Sun-Times, the Chicago American and the Daily News. And, there are three daily editions of each. Every morning, afternoon and evening, there is a new edition of current news.

"Why is the money just laying there in the open?"

"It's the honor system. People take a paper and leave the money on the table. Some days, it is how I survive if my dad doesn't come home."

"What do you mean?"

"Watch."

As they walked by, without missing a step or slowing down, Ed quickly flashed his hand over the corner of the table and scooped up some change. Once they crossed the street, he counted it.

"Great, thirty-two cents." He said with a smile.

"Papa, that's stealing!"

"Yeah, I know. It's not right, but understand that tonight I will go home to a basement with a cot and no refrigerator, or anything, really. I would bet a nickel that my dad won't come home, so I'm on my own. It's how I survived sometimes."

"Aren't you scared?" LeeAnn asked in concern.

"Nah. In fact I'm more afraid if my dad does come home. Most times he's drunk and he's mean." Papa stated casually.

"Does he hit you?"

Papa laughed. "Oh yeah!

"Can't you call someone?" LeeAnn asked.

"Sweetie, in 1956, there was no one to call. Children had no rights at all. Everybody gets to take a swing at us. Parents, teachers, police…most any authority can whack you a good one."

"I'm so sorry, Papa." LeeAnn said sadly.

"I'm not sure whether you can understand, but it isn't all that bad. Let me ask you; how many kids do you know that are on medication, or have been diagnosed with A.D.D.?"

"I know a few." She answered quickly.

"All I can tell you is that a paddle or strap can instantly cure a lot of those diseases. Show me a healthy active child with a good imagination and they all have A.D.D.! One has to learn how to concentrate and study. In fact, I have double A.D.D. if I can get away with it!"

"What good is the thirty-two cents you stole?" LeeAnn scoffed.

"With twenty-five cents, I can get a hot dog and French fries—and, if I buy my pop over at the Pepsi truck garage, it is only a nickel. So thirty cents is dinner!"

"You are kidding me!"

"Nope! Everything is a whole lot cheaper in 1956. I think you will find this journey not only educational, but quite fun. Plus, I will have a few pennies to pitch."

"What does that mean?"

Ed smiled. "I'll show you after school. It's another way that I can make a little money."

Now they were walking down a side street, and were passing little houses, called bungalows, that Chicago was known for. They are small family homes, built with large front porches. Most had swing or gliders and lawn type chairs, and she noticed most furniture was wooden. To LeeAnn, they appeared a bit strange, for none of these houses were at ground level. They all had five or six steps up to the front door.

"Are these apartments?" She wondered.

"No. They have basements, but actually half the basements are above ground level. That raises the house about four feet off the ground." He explained.

"Why?"

"I think it was so basements could have windows and not be like caves. In the really old days, it was likely because they needed to get coal into the basements and needed a coal chute. In fact, the building my mom lives in still uses coal for their furnace."

"Coal? Like charcoal for a cookout?"

He realized that likely she had never seen coal. "No, it is very different. It is like a black rock, except it is a bit softer and oily if you handle it. It burns much faster and hotter than charcoal. You'll know it if you see it or handle it, because it smells, and will leave a black soot on your hands."

Soon they were in front of the school. The first thing LeeAnn noticed was the nuns in their black habits, or uniforms. The children were gathering in groups and beginning to form lines.

"What do I do?"

"Just follow me."

"Those are nuns?" She asked.

"Yeah, they are Dominicans, as far their order. They are pretty tough, but the Franciscans are the worst I have met up with so far. There are no nice nuns! They are all meaner than sh--, I mean, crap."

LeeAnn giggled, because she knew that Papa always had a habit slipping and using swears now and then. She followed along and got in line. She was nervous, as she knew nothing of what to expect and hoped she could just get in and out without being noticed. It was obvious that the lines were separated by boys and girls. As she entered the girls' line, Papa whispered "Not to worry, this is my world and you are only a spectator."

Hearing that, LeeAnn relaxed a bit, but it was then a nun looked at her and sternly said "Miss LeeAnn, straighten those stockings!"

'*Great! I thought Papa said it was his dream!*' She thought. LeeAnn began to worry about what would come next? Then she heard the nun scream. "Eddie! Eddie Burk! You cut that out!"

LeeAnn held her breath as she followed the line into the school. Everything was so quiet and orderly. She became anxious for what would come next?

Chapter Two

As LeeAnn entered the classroom, she was impressed at how neat and orderly things were. All the students proceeded immediately to their desks, quickly and quietly. She only had to lag slightly behind before her open seat became obvious. She found the desks to be very different than what she was accustomed to, as these desks were bolted to the floor with a straight back and an immoveable seat that forced everyone to sit up straight. She followed the example the class gave as all the students sat silently with both hands folded atop their desks. The nun was a peculiar sight, as her habit [outfit] of black flowing robes almost made it appear that she was hovering above the floor. The starched white collar and head cover reinforced her stern expression. *'I guess I would look unhappy if I had to wear that outfit, too. What if her head ever itches?'* LeeAnn wondered. As the nun moved to the front of the room, she made the eighteen inch ruler in her hand look like a potential weapon, which LeeAnn would soon learn it actually was.

"Good morning children."

The classroom answered in unison. "Good morning Sister Bernice."

She asked, "Helen, will you lead us in the Pledge of Allegiance?" Everyone knew she was asking, but also understood it was a direct order. While the class recited the Pledge of Allegiance, LeeAnn examined the slot shelf under the top of the desk. It was filled with books. *'Geez, how many books do they have?'* She wondered, as she stood with her hand covering her heart. When the class finished, Sister Bernice continued.

"Thomas, will you lead us in prayer?"

LeeAnn mimicked the rest of the class as they sat with their hands folded in prayer, with heads tilted downward. Thomas began.

"Our Father, who art in Heaven......"

As the class joined in reverently, she inconspicuously examined the books since her head was tilted downward. What first caught her eye was a huge history book, about three inches thick. Next to it was a large English book. She glanced upward and saw the large map of the United

States pulled down over a portion of the chalkboard, which covered two walls of the classroom. As Thomas finished the Lord's Prayer, he began saying the Hail Mary, which was a prayer LeeAnn had never heard. She found praying in school a strange experience, as this was not allowed in her school. She also noticed the large crucifix high on wall in the front of the room. What impressed her was that all the students seemed so serious, and there was no talking.

LeeAnn smiled at the girl next to her, who smiled back. When she turned her head, Sister Bernice barked loudly. "LeeAnn pay attention!" LeeAnn realized that this was very different than what she was used to. In 2010, sometimes the teacher was not even in the room and assignments were just written on the board. In fact, she found the boards strange, as they were all chalkboards with a small shelf holding erasers and chalk. Plus, there was no talking at all! In her 2010 classroom, talking to each other was not a problem. She was shocked when Sister Bernice scurried down the row and whacked a boy on the head with a ruler.

"Bobby, you know what you did!"

"Yes, Sister." He said timidly.

"Bobby has something so important to say that he is sending notes. Bobby, why don't you read what was so important that it could not wait for recess?"

Bobby stood up and unfolded a small piece of paper. He swallowed hard and quietly read out loud. "Let's go swimming after school."

LeeAnn could see the little beads of sweat forming on Bobby's forehead. She watched as Sister Bernice grabbed the note.

"Let me see that! So, 'let's go swimming after school' is urgent? Look at this poor penmanship! This looks as if it were written by a second grader!" She handed the note back to Bobby.

Sister Bernice then whacked her palm with the ruler, making a loud snapping sound. "Bobby, that just did not seem like it was all that important. I think it could have even waited until lunch. So, will you fold it up and eat it please!" She ordered.

LeeAnn watched in shock as Bobby folded up the little piece of paper and put it in his mouth and began chewing. *'Oh my God!'* LeeAnn thought.

The nun seemed to glide back to the front of the room. "Joyce, please stand?"

The girl that LeeAnn smiled at stood straight in the isle. "Yes, Sister." She said confidently.

The nun picked up a pointer and walked to the huge map. "Can you identify the places I point to, please?" She pointed and as she did, Joyce quickly gave the answers without any hesitation.

"Pacific Ocean, Sister. Atlantic Ocean, Sister. Oklahoma, Sister. Canada, Sister. Mexico, Sister."

Sister Bernice smiled with approval. "Thank you, Joyce."

"Bobby, Mister paper eater...Who warned us that the British were coming?"

Bobby stood up and responded quickly. "Paul Revere, Sister."

"And who said 'I regret I only have one life to give for my country?"

"Nathan Hale, Sister." Bobby replied.

"Eddie Burk, who made the first American flag?"

Ed stood up quickly. "Betsy Ross, Sister Bernice."

"And what is so important about 1776?"

"It is the year we declared independence from the British, Sister." Ed responded.

"You can sit down, Mr. Burk."

"Very good, children. Maybe we did learn something this year. Next year I will be turning you over to Sister Fabiola, and I want all of you to represent me well! As all of you know, today is a half day and I would like to collect all the books. You have all written your names in pencil inside the cover, so please erase your name. Bobby Mack and Eddie Burk will collect them. Boys, you can stack them on the table right here. We'll start with the history books."

LeeAnn was amazed as she pulled out the huge history book and it had her name on the inside cover. She quickly erased it as instructed. Her Papa grinned as he added her book to the pile and set the stack in the front of the room on the table. Since the table was behind where the nun was standing, Papa Ed started making faces and arm gestures behind her back. This brought giggles from the whole class. Sister Bernice spun around and caught him making a weird expression. "Oh, it seems we have a clown in our class! I guess I will have to warn Sister Fabiola she is in for some humor next year! Now, Eddie Burk, show us your funniest face."

With that being said, he did as ordered and made stupid grin. As the class laughed, LeeAnn was stunned as Sister Bernice slammed the ruler on his head! "Now collect the English books, but before you do, recite the vowels please."

Papa Ed smiled. "A,E,I,O,U and sometimes Y."

"Very good, my little comedian!" She barked.

LeeAnn hesitantly reached into the desk shelf. Sure enough, there was an English book with her name penciled in. This book was smaller, but still a few inches thick. One by one, she surrendered her books, all which were inscribed with her name. Civics, music, history, English, arithmetic and even Catechism, a book she had never heard of. This was amazing, for in 2010, she had NO books! She also held her breath and was anxious that Sister Bernice might call on her. It seemed they had learned far beyond what she had learned so far in her classes. Sister Bernice began writing fractions on the chalkboard and then turned and ordered. "Michael White, can you come up here and solve this for me?"

'*Fractions? We haven't had these yet?*' LeeAnn watched as Michael easily converted the numbers into the correct answer. As he finished, a bell rang loudly. LeeAnn thought this would signal a stampede to recess, but instead everyone sat with hands folded. Sister Bernice gave the class a pleased expression. "You may leave for recess." She stated. The children got up, and in an orderly fashion they all left the room. Some headed for the washrooms, other drifted out to the playground. Once outside, she breathed a sigh of relief. Her Papa walked up. "The boys really don't talk much to the girls, so I'll see you after school." Before she could say 'Pa--', he was gone and throwing a baseball to another boy. Joyce walked up to her.

"I know we don't know each other well, but would you like to play after school?"

LeeAnn was confused, as what she should, or even could, do. "I think I may have to go home and change out of these clothes."

"Well, can we meet at Wilson's Drug store; let's say at one o'clock?"

LeeAnn was hesitant, but agreed. "Okay. But what will we do?"

"We can have a cherry Coke and then go to the record store and listen to some cool new music. You know, Rock and Roll!"

"Uh? Okay." '*Record store? Rock and Roll?*' LeeAnn wondered.

"Want to play jacks?" Joyce asked.

"Jacks?" LeeAnn repeated.

"Don't tell me you have never played Jacks." Joyce replied.

"Uh, not really. I know what they are."

"Okay, how about hopscotch?"

"Uh, I don't know that very well either." LeeAnn replied.

Joyce was drawing a blank. "Paddle ball?" She asked.

LeeAnn shook her head negative.

"Okay, let's just go sit on the swings and watch them do jump rope."

LeeAnn was not sure exactly what jump rope was and as they sat on the swings, she watched as two girls swung a huge jump rope in a large loop and a third hopped into the middle and began jumping and skipping rhythmically all the while reciting a rhyme. *'Cool'* she thought.

"Do you have the latest Elvis record?" Joyce asked.

"No." LeeAnn answered.

"Well we'll hear it at the record store. He's going to be on Ed Sullivan, you know."

LeeAnn faked it. "Yeah, I can't wait." She had heard of Elvis, but who was Ed Sullivan?

"I heard they will only show him from the waist up." Joyce laughed.

"Why?" LeeAnn was curious.

"They said the way he moves and dances is immoral and dirty."

"Oh." LeeAnn responded. *'My God, wait until they see Demi Lovato or Rihanna.'*

She looked around, and although strange, it appeared the kids were generally happier than she was normally used to seeing. Almost everyone was smiling and she heard no swears, not even from the bigger kids. She noticed there was little or no supervision necessary. She also noticed they were absolutely no electronics. She saw no iPods, MP3 players, radios, or anything else. Instead, aside from a few kids talking, most were moving about, playing various sports. The boys were playing baseball, basketball, football and even marbles. The girls were playing volleyball, tetherball, jump rope and she reasoned that the girls hopping about on chalk drawn squares must be playing hopscotch. Everyone seemed so happy and carefree, and no one seemed stressed. Just then, the bell rang and they made their way into the lines entering the school. Once at her desk, with hands folded, she watched the clock. *'Great! A few more hours of this...'* Was her first thought.

Sister Bernice was sitting at her desk smiling. "Just a reminder, children; the school library will be open all summer and I have a list of books that Sister Fabiola will assign you to read next year. So for those that would like to get ahead, you'll have plenty of time to read on vacation. I will also be giving you a list of approved movies that you can see, should your parents take you. As the boys collect the music books, can we all sing the America the Beautiful, please?" Sister Bernice pulled out a little round tuning instrument from under her smock and blew into it. It sounded a bit like a harmonica, but only sounded one note. It was the key to begin. The whole class began singing enthusiastically. "**Oh beautiful, for spacious skies...**"

As they sang, LeeAnn pondered the nun's comment. *'Approved movies? What's that?'*

When they finished singing, Sister Bernice announced. "Let me hear the multiplication tables starting from one through twelve. Each of you will recite a number going alphabetically. Johnny Adams, please start." Johnny stood up grinning, because his was easy. "One times one is one, one times two is two..." When he finished, the next student began. At seven, it was Papa's turn. "Eddie Burk?" Sister Bernice called.

LeeAnn watched as he stood with confidence and rolled off the multiplication table with no effort, finishing with "Seven times twelve equals eighty-four." Fortunately for LeeAnn, they finished at twelve before it was her turn. She breathed a sigh of relief.

"Very Good children! Sister Fabiola will be pleased to have this class next year." What LeeAnn did not know, was that Sister Bernice's teaching skills would be judged by the nun--in this case Sister Fabiola, when she inherited this class. Sister Bernice had put all her efforts into preparing this class for the next level as they would reflect her teaching ability. "When I call your name, please come and get your final report card. I urge those of you that need help in certain subjects to use your vacation time to your advantage. Johnny Adams, let's get started."

One by one she called their names, including LeeAnn's. Just as in her real life, she had also gotten straight A's in this life as well. When she was done, the nun stood in front of the class, and for the first time, LeeAnn saw Sister Bernice smile. "I am pleased with all of you children. I have enjoyed working with all of you, and hope that you all continue to progress. If I could get a volunteer to clean the erasers, I think we are about finished. I know it's a bit early, but this fine class deserves it. I am proud of each and every one of you. I hope to see all of you at church on Sundays, and I hope you all have a great and safe summer. Congratulations to you, new fifth graders. God be with each of you. You may go!"

Instead of mass chaos, the students stood slowly. As if rehearsed, each went to Sister Bernice, and one by one, gave her a hug or shook her hand, thanking her. LeeAnn followed the routine and gave her a hug and thanked her. Afterward, she followed Joyce outside. She watched as a boy carried out a pile of erasers and began banging them together, creating a huge white cloud of chalk dust.

"I'm going home to get changed." LeeAnn told Joyce. Meanwhile, she was keeping an eye on Papa Ed, who was standing and waiting for her.

"Well, I'll see you at Wilson's at one." Joyce reminded her.

"Okay, I'll be there." She walked over to Papa. "I guess I should go home and change."

"Yeah, I'll walk you."

"Where is Wilson's?" LeeAnn asked.

"We will pass it on the way home. It's a drug store. However, in 1956, most of them have what is called 'soda fountains' where they serve ice cream and make soda pop. Wilson's makes great Green River." He replied.

'Green River? I guess this where Papa developed his taste for it.' She knew her grandpa loved Green River, and 2010, it was not widely distributed, so he ordered it from a specialty house on the internet. Everyone in the family knew never to touch Papa's Green River.

"I'm supposed to meet Joyce there after I get changed. Will you go with me?"

It was obvious that she was insecure. "Yeah, I'll walk you there, but then I'm going to pitch some pennies." He answered.

"Pitch pennies? What is that?"

"It's fun, and it's my way of making a little money. Sometimes, we even pitch nickels." He bragged.

"What is it?" LeeAnn asked again.

"When you come out of Wilson's, just look across the street and you'll see me. Come over and watch. Here..." He handed her a quarter. "You'll need this."

"But Papa, all you have is thirty-two cents."

"Don't worry about me, I'll be fine."

"If my mom is working, who will be home? How can I just leave? Won't she be angry?" LeeAnn worried.

"Nah. This is 1956. Kids our age go about freely during the daytime. Besides, you are just going around the neighborhood. You can go to the swimming pool which is indoors, and likely your mom will want you to run errands and go to the store on your own anyway."

"I never get to go out alone." LeeAnn responded.

"Never?" Papa Ed repeated.

"No. I could never just go out to a store by myself."

"I guess that's a huge difference in the times. You see, we have never even heard the term 'predator' in our day. I actually never heard of such a thing as a child molester. In 1956, we did not worry about such things. Walking around the city, the only worry I might have is running into an occasional bully. This will be very different for you. During this time, your parents will almost expect you to go outside and travel the neighborhood, or go by yourself to the store and get bread or milk."

"You're kidding!"

"No, I'm not. The only thing kids are going home early for is to watch the Mickey Mouse Club, which is a great new TV program. Even the boys run home to see Annette!"

"Who is Annette?"

"Annette is the prettiest Mouseketeer!"

"Really?"

"Sure. In 1956, Disney ruled. He has the Mickey Mouse Club, plus Disney specials on Sundays, and he even opened Disneyland this year."

"You mean Disneyworld." LeeAnn corrected.

"No. Disneyworld is not even thought of yet. Today, we only have Disneyland in California. Plus, we have all the great Disney movies such as Peter Pan, Davey Crockett, Lady and the Tramp—just to name a few; plus great comic books!"

"Well, we're here. I'll go up and change."

"You do that and I'll meet you back here in about twenty minutes."

She watched and he took off running down the block. Up the stairs she traveled, and was surprised when the front door was unlocked. It was obvious that her mom was not home yet. She went to her room and changed from her dress into denim jeans and a top that looked shirt-like. She watched the clock and realized she had time to examine this new world. She went to the front room and turned on the television. She laughed at the small screen and quickly realized that there was no remote. Instead, there was a huge dial with only 12 numbers. It was already on number five, so she turned it on and watched as it warmed up and gradually produced a blurry picture that was black and white. She noticed a huge antenna was setting on the top, so she moved it a bit and the picture became much clearer. Being it was still within the lunch hour, a children's program was on and it was a man called 'Uncle Johnny Coons.' She laughed out loud at the fact that he talked to the kids as though they were all five year olds. He used some hand puppets that were really obvious and lame. *'What a dork.'* She could see the microphone over his head, and reasoned that this was a 'live' show. *'Weird.'*

She changed the channel to number nine and stopped when she saw a huge obese man in a pirate suit. *'This is bizarre.'* It was another children's show and he proudly proclaimed he was "Two Ton Baker, the music maker!" She stepped back and was amazed that this little picture was contained in such a huge furniture cabinet. On top of the television was a guide, and she looked it over. There was nothing she recognized as she read off the programs.

"Howdy Doody? Ray Rayner? Lorretta Young? Sid Ceasar?" As she looked about, the huge black telephone caught her attention. Slowly, she walked over and saw it had a rotary dial and no push buttons. *'Nothing is digital?'* She noticed in the center of the dial was a number. AR 7-2675. *'Could that be our phone number? Where is the area code?'* She wondered.

Hesitantly, she lifted the heavy receiver off its cradle. Just as she had been told, it was a party line, and she could hear two women having a conversation. She was so very tempted to make a farting sound, but thought it better not to. Instead she quietly set it down. *'Just like Papa said.'*

She knew Papa would be back soon, so she went downstairs and decided to investigate the delicatessen. It had a strange smell, and two walls lined with refrigerated meat cases. Immediately she noticed the vast variety of lunch meats and salads. Mister Waluska greeted her.

"Hello young lady. Can I help you?"

LeeAnn smiled politely. "No thank you. I was just looking at all this lunch meat."

He smiled and bragged. "We have the largest selection in the neighborhood."

"What is this one?" She asked as she pointed.

"Well, let me go down the first row. We have Olive loaf, pimento loaf, veal bologna, salami, pastrami, garlic bologna, head cheese, meatloaf, and three grades of roast beef, corned beef, turkey, plain bologna, Polish ham, smoked ham, boiled ham, liver sausage, Italian salami, and spiced ham. This is just the first row."

LeeAnn noticed what looked to be some dead fish that were near yellow in color. "What are those?"

"That's smoked fish. Would you like a taste?" He asked.

"Uh, no thanks."

"How about a sample of something else? Come on, I'll cut you a slice." He offered.

"Okay, maybe a slice of ham?"

"Which one, honey?" He asked.

"How about the Polish ham." She picked it because she knew Papa always asked for Polish hams when anyone traveled from Chicago, as it was not available in the Ozarks. She was always curious, and Mister Waluska was anxious to please her.

"Could I make you a small sandwich?"

"No, thank you. A slice will be fine." She watched as he shaved off a thin slice, setting it on a piece of white butcher's paper and handing it to her.

When she tasted it, her eyes widened and she said "Wow! This is good!"

"I'll tell your mom you like it and maybe she will buy it the next time she comes in."

LeeAnn headed for the door. "Thank you!" she exclaimed as she wandered onto the sidewalk and observed the store fronts. There were little shops everywhere. It was almost like some kind of a theme park, like the shops at Silver Dollar City. As she just stared, she realized there was a man standing behind her, which startled her. She turned quickly and realized it was a policeman.

"Sorry if I scared you honey. You look like you're lost. Is everything okay?"

LeeAnn smiled. "Yes, Officer. I am just waiting for my Pa…um, friend."

"Well, I walk this neighborhood, and if anyone bothers you, you just holler." He smiled as he walked away, whistling.

She laughed to herself, because she knew she really was lost, but there was no way he could ever imagine how lost she actually was. She walked to the corner of the busy intersection and noticed people sitting patiently on a bench, waiting for a bus that was coming up the street in their direction. Around the corner was a marquee that was advertizing "The Wolfman and Dracula" in lights. It was an old movie theater. There was a ticket booth right on the street in front of the entrance, and the smell of popcorn filled the air. She walked up to the ticket booth.

"How much is a ticket?"

"It's a double feature, and for kids it's ten cents."

"Ten cents?" She repeated in wonder.

"That's what I said, but you get to see both movies!" He boasted.

"How many screens do you have?" LeeAnn asked as if expecting a multiplex theater.

He gave her a strange look and answered. "One."

There was no such thing as theaters having more than one screen and double features were shown back to back, one after the other. He scratched his head and asked. "Is there a theater you know of that has more than one screen?"

"Uh, no. I guess it was a dumb question." She offered in explanation. She turned and went back around the corner and saw Papa waiting at her doorstep.

"You're not getting in trouble are you?" He asked, seeing her confused expression.

"No, but I did forget myself for a moment."

"Easy to do, so be very careful. People might get the impression that you are an alien or something!" He laughed.

"They are showing two movies for ten cents. I couldn't believe it."

"Yeah, and both are black and white. That is a small theater that only shows the older releases. On Saturday, they will show twenty cartoons, Flash Gordon, and two movies, plus a huge bag of popcorn, all for twenty cents."

"No way." LeeAnn replied in awe.

"Yeah way! This is 1956. Come on let's go."

He led the way to Wilson's drug store.

"I guess policemen just walk around?" She asked.

"Yes, they do. They also drive around in cars, but in busier areas they patrol on foot."

"Is there that much crime?" LeeAnn asked logically.

"No way. Did you take a close look at him? If it was Officer Finn, he weighs over 200 pounds. Who is he going to catch? Mostly, he hassles the teenagers that gather around the corner or in front of certain stores. He doesn't take any crap either. He will not hesitate kicking you in the butt if he feels like it."

"I thought he was nice."

'He's okay, I guess."

"I tasted Polish ham!" She bragged. "And Papa, that store must have had a hundred kinds of lunch meat!"

"In 1956, each store owner was a lot nicer. Kids like us could eat free all day just by walking the neighborhoods. Unlike 2010, most stores are actually managed by the owners. Owners tend to be friendlier and kinder, and more anxious to please their customers. We do have some larger stores. We have a Sears further north, and a Montgomery Ward downtown, along with a Marshall Field's, but my favorite is Goldblatt's."

"I heard of Sears, but not the others."

"Yeah, I forgot. They're gone now. Well not now, but...you know... Here's Wilson's!" Papa announced. "You got the quarter?"

LeeAnn nodded positive.

"Have fun. I'll be across the street pitching."

She still didn't know what he was talking about as far as pitching, but she nodded. "Okay."

LeeAnn walked into Wilson's and looked around. To her, it looked like an old fashioned drug store. In the back was something she had never seen before, however, which was a soda fountain. It was a long counter made of beautiful marble and lined in front with swivel stools of red leather. There, sat Joyce. LeeAnn walked up timidly with a smile. Joyce happened to be dressed nearly identical, in jeans, a shirt like top, and loafers. "Let's try cherry Coke!" She suggested.

"Okay"

A young man dressed in all in white took their order and LeeAnn watched as he poured syrup in each glass and then added cherry flavoring. When he finished, he put each glass under the fountain and added carbonated water and stirred them with a spoon. He carefully placed a napkin on the counter and set the glasses down. "That will be ten cents."

"For both?" LeeAnn asked.

"Yes, for both." He replied with a smile.

She looked at Joyce, smiling. "My treat!" She set her quarter down and he delivered her change. She noticed a huge brass cash register, and he had to press various keys to eventually get it to ring and get the cash drawer open. *'Weird!'* she thought.

"Thanks!" Joyce grinned. Then her smile faded. Looking a bit hesitant, she then questioned LeeAnn. "You seem like you are not from here. Can I ask where you are from?"

LeeAnn saw no problem in telling her. "I came here from Missouri."

"Is it a lot different?" Joyce wondered.

"Uh, yeah. For sure!" LeeAnn thought Joyce could never understand exactly how different it really was.

"What is the biggest difference?" Joyce asked.

LeeAnn, again, did not have a problem answering with the truth. "Well, stuff costs more, and we don't have the same things you do here."

"Yeah, Chicago has everything. WJJD--our record station--plays a lot of Rock and Roll, and broadcasts across the nation. I have a cousin in

Iowa, and he says we get all the new music months before he gets it in his town!"

LeeAnn thought it best to play ignorant. "I really never listen to music that much."

"Yeah, some parents are like that. Some of the churches don't approve of the new music. Do your parents allow it?"

"Uh, well I really don't have my own radio."

"I don't either, but my mom lets me play my channel at times. Have you ever been here before? For fifteen cents they make the best chocolate sodas. In fact, if you just get the soda without the ice cream it's only ten cents. It's called a chocolate phosphate. It's really good."

LeeAnn was curious. "Do your parents let you travel around by yourself?"

"Yeah, as long as it's light outside and I'm home for dinner. In fact, if my mom wants time alone or has friends over, she sends me out to play."

"What do you do?" LeeAnn wondered.

"Usually I go see if my friends can come out, or just ride my bike to the park."

"Don't you worry that bad people might uh…bother you?" LeeAnn asked.

"Like who? What do you mean by 'bad' people?"

"Like being kidnapped or something?"

Joyce laughed. "You mean like in the movies or something? Why would you think like that?"

"Uh, I just wondered because my parents are so strict about me going out alone."

"Missouri must be a dangerous place." Joyce assumed. "No, no one would ever bother me. It's just the opposite. If I hang upside down on the monkey bars, people will yell that I might get hurt. The only thing I ever hear is to watch myself crossing the busy streets."

LeeAnn thought long and hard about that. *'Wouldn't it be nice to walk anywhere without worrying about predators?'* She wondered what it would be like to just travel about without any constraints. *'This is kind of awesome.'*

"Let's go listen to some music!" Joyce suggested.

"Okay!" As they walked out of Wilson's, LeeAnn could see her Papa across the street with a group of boys doing something and being loud, like cheering each other on. "Can we go see what they are doing?"

Joyce giggled. "Oh, those are the boys just pitching pennies. They may not like it much if we linger there too long, but we can look."

They crossed the street and about eight boys were gathered. As she watched, the sidewalk was divided with lines that defined squares every three feet or so. The boys lined up behind a line and then one by one they tossed a penny at the line two squares away. She quickly figured out that closest penny to the line won all the money. Finally, it was Papa's turn. He glanced at LeeAnn and winked. He tossed his penny right on the line. "Guess I win, suckers!" He scoffed.

"Burk, that's it for me." One boy replied.

"Come on! Let's do at least one for a nickel?" Papa asked.

Two of the boys stepped up. "Let's do it."

As LeeAnn watched, the first boy tossed his and it rolled a foot away from the line. She heard him say "Ah, shit…" to himself. The second boy carefully tossed his and it landed only an inch from the line. "Beat that Burk." He challenged.

Papa stepped up and slowly swung his arm forward. At first, it appeared his was a bad toss as it landed a foot away, but as everyone watched, it continued sliding forward and landed right in the crack. "Anyone else feel lucky?" Papa challenged.

"Up yours, Burk." One boy spat.

"Hey! Money talks and bullshit walks." Papa shot back. He then remembered LeeAnn was there and put his hand over his mouth. "Sorry girls."

"Come on LeeAnn, let's go listen to some new records." Joyce urged, frowning. "Those boys sometimes use the worst language. If Sister Bernice ever heard that, she would whack them good!"

Based on what LeeAnn experienced, that was an understatement! A few doors down was the record store. It was very strange. It had isles with tubs of records on long tables, all in alphabetical order by artist. There was hardly an artist she had ever heard of? Who was Frankie Lane, or Doris Day? In a section labeled Rock and Roll, again she was stumped. Who was Gene Vincent, or The Crickets, or Chuck Berry? On the walls of the store, besides pictures of record artists, were also some guitars hanging that were for sale. Joyce quickly went to the Elvis section and pulled out what was a 45 RPM record. LeeAnn actually thought it was huge. *'Much larger than a CD. It must have a lot of songs on it.'* She thought.

"How many songs are on that?" LeeAnn asked.

"Two silly! One on the front and one on the back."

LeeAnn noticed it had a big hole in the middle. '*Strange!*'

Joyce guided her to a booth that was sound proof, but had a glass window so people could see in. In the room was a turntable, and she watched as Joyce grabbed a small adapter and snapped it into the larger hole on the record, allowing it to spin on the turntable. She handed LeeAnn the headphones and set the arm down on the record. The song was "Don't Be Cruel." LeeAnn had never heard it before, but it sounded like many of the oldies she had heard played. "Now tell me that's not the coolest!" Joyce raved. '*So this is the great Elvis.*' She thought, and found her foot tapping.

LeeAnn looked about and saw some larger records being handled out in the store. "How many songs are on those big records?" She asked.

"Oh, those are the old 78's, they only have two songs on them also. But they're on the way out and 45's are in."

LeeAnn just smiled. '*Wait till she has an M3P player, she will freak out!*'

"They are making new record players now, where you can put a whole stack of records on and they will play continuously. My parents have one, but it will only do it with the old 78's. My friend had a portable record player and he brings it to the park."

"So it runs on batteries?" LeeAnn assumed.

"No, it is a wind up." Joyce laughed.

"A wind up?"

"Yeah, it has a crank and you wind it and it plays a record. It is not very loud, but it sounds okay."

LeeAnn had seen enough in this day to be completely amazed. As Joyce listened to the record, she watched the people and noticed the boys seemed to have only two hair styles. Some had their hair short with the tops cut almost perfectly flat, and others had their hair long and kind of greasy looking. Most all were wearing denim and had tee shirts with the short sleeves rolled up, showing all their arms. She had to laugh, because some had arms so skinny it looked silly. She asked Joyce.

"The boys with long hair comb it straight back on the sides to where it meets in the back and they don't comb the back of their hair straight down. What is that?"

"They call it a D-A." Joyce replied.

"What's a D-A?" LeeAnn asked.

Joyce leaned close and whispered. "It stands for ducks ass."

LeeAnn laughed. "You're kidding me."

"No, a lot of them that think they are hoods comb their hair that way."

"Hoods?"

"Yeah. It's short for hoodlum. They think they are cool. When it gets colder, you will spot them by their leather jackets. See that guy over there?"

He looked to be about thirteen or fourteen. "Under his rolled up sleeve you can see his cigarettes."

"He can have cigarettes?" LeeAnn was shocked.

"Yeah, lot's of the kids here smoke."

At that moment, LeeAnn noticed the man at the register smoking, and also an older boy with a cigarette hanging out of his mouth, thumbing through the records. "Smoking is bad for you…" LeeAnn stated.

Joyce just looked at her confused. "Says who?"

LeeAnn realized it was 1956. "Well, it can't be good breathing in smoke. Will you ever smoke?"

"My mom says I have to be at least fourteen. Some doctors say it is very relaxing."

'*Very relaxing? Oh my God! Doctors? Man are they in for a surprise!'* LeeAnn thought to herself.

As she listened to the music, LeeAnn lost herself in the moment and began dancing, doing some subtle moving.

"What are you doing?" Joyce laughed.

"Oh, I'm just dancing a little." LeeAnn answered.

"You can't dance by yourself!" Joyce explained. "You always must have a partner. Don't you ever watch Bandstand?"

"Uh, no." LeeAnn answered but was confused by the whole dancing discussion. In 1956, no one danced without touching and holding a partner. Even the new Be-Bop dancing was just a form of the Jitterbug of the forties. Standing alone and moving in an uncoordinated manner made one look odd in 1956, if not a bit crazy.

"You must watch Bandstand. They have a new guy hosting and his name is Dick Clark. He is really cute! They play all the latest records and do the latest dances. Way better than the Hit Parade show, which is mainly for the adults, anyway." Joyce related. Joyce glanced at the clock. "Want to come to my house and watch the Mickey Mouse club?"

"LeeAnn thought a moment. "Uh, no I better not, because I really don't know when my mom gets home. I want to be there. So, maybe tomorrow?"

"Okay. I'm going to get going, so I'll see you tomorrow."

As they left the store, and Joyce walked away, LeeAnn realized that she did not know Joyce's phone number, or even where she lived? She knew the way back to her apartment, but looked around for Papa. Just down the street coming out of a garage door she saw him walking out drinking a Pepsi in a glass bottle.

"Having fun?" He asked.

"Papa, I find this amazing."

"Yeah, the world was more of an adventure for children during this era. It seemed everyday was a new surprise. From food, to music, to clothes, it seemed each year brought great new things. I actually had a bad childhood by most standards, but I have fond memories of being on my own in this city." He explained.

"I got a bit embarrassed." LeeAnn admitted.

"Why?"

"Well, we were listening to music, and I started dancing a bit, and Joyce looked at me as if I was crazy." LeeAnn explained.

Papa laughed. "Yeah, that isn't done. That type of dancing really didn't become popular until the sixties. Today, people would think you were retarded or had some kind of physical disorder! Big deal. She thinks you're a spaz. So what?"

"Great! Joyce thinks I'm a spazzola!" LeeAnn laughed. "So? What's next?" She asked.

"Well, I think you should go home and watch the Mickey Mouse Club like the rest of the world. Spend some time with your mom and dad." He suggested.

As they talked, a bus went by and LeeAnn just stared at the rod on the back going up and connecting to a huge electric wire, which was hanging over the street.

"I love those buses." Papa stated. "See the bumper on the back? I can jump on and hold onto that rod and ride all over the city for free."

"You're kidding?" LeeAnn stated.

"Want to know the strangest thing? In 2010, they are talking about bringing them back!"

"You're kidding me!" LeeAnn replied, and looked for the expression that Papa was about to tell one of his whoppers.

"No, no lie. They are realizing that they are clean as far as emissions, and are more energy efficient. Everything old is new again!" He laughed.

"Come outside after dinner and we can tour some more. I'll see you later."

As she watched, he took off running and jumped on the back of the bus. As it proceeded down the street, he held on with one hand and waved goodbye with the other, flashing his all too familiar smile.

"That was awesome!" LeeAnn looked about and proceeded walking home. She felt excited that this adventure would continue.

Chapter Three

LeeAnn made her way up the stairs, and once again the door was unlocked, which she found so unusual. As she entered, her mom greeted her. "Hello dear! I already put your favorite program on the TV. You made it just in time."

LeeAnn was surprised, and went in to see exactly what her favorite program was.

As she entered the front room, she could hear the song *"M-I-C, K-E-Y, M-O-U-S-E."* She knew it had to be the Mickey Mouse Club. She sat mesmerized, knowing she was watching history. Papa was correct; out of all the Mouseketeers, Annette was the most beautiful…but it was little Cubby that caught her eye. *'He's so cute!'* As she watched, her mom brought her some chocolate milk and cookies.

"Here, Sweetie."

She took a big sip of the milk, and it was better than she had ever tasted. "What kind of chocolate milk is this, mom?"

"Oh, it's just milk mixed with Bosco, as always. You said you liked it better than Ovaltine." She answered.

'What the heck is Bosco? What is Ovaltine?'

What began as mere curiosity became instant enjoyment, as even though the singing and dancing was dated, each segment was enjoyable and even educational. LeeAnn was glued to the black and white television and when the program went into the finale, she felt sad it was over. The end of the song "M-I-C--see you real soon! K-E-Y--why? Because we like you! M-O-U-S-E.!" This melody just kept repeating in her head and she was anxious to see another episode.

She picked up her plate and the empty glass, and walked to the kitchen where her mom was busy cooking dinner.

"Smells great, Mom. What is it?"

"Oh, it is a new recipe I found in a magazine. It is a chicken casserole. Would you do me a favor and take out the garbage please?"

"Uh, sure. Where is it?"

Her mom looked at her strangely. "Under the sink, where it always is."

LeeAnn looked under the sink, which had no cabinet. There sat a paper bag. She picked it up and remembered what Papa had told her, that the garbage cans were in back of buildings in the so-called alleys. So out she went through the back door onto the porch, where next door sat an older woman on a porch swing. "Hi honey."

"Hi." LeeAnn responded.

"My name is Jeanne, and I heard all about you. You must be LeeAnn. My husband told me you loved the taste of Polish ham."

LeeAnn reasoned that this had to be Mister Waluska's wife. "Yes, it was delicious."

"Well, I'll have my Ed bring your mom a pound or so, just to try." She offered.

"Thank you!"

"You are such a good girl, taking out the garbage for your mom."

Seeing as that the bag she was carrying was no bigger than a grocery bag, she decided to offer. "Do you have any garbage for me to take down? It's no trouble."

"No thank you, Honey, but so kind of you to offer. See these over here?" She was pointing at some empty pop and beer bottles setting on her porch. "You can have these if you like."

LeeAnn's mind was flashing and deducting. Assuming she had nothing to throw out, then those bottles must have some value? "Uh, thank you. I...I may take a few later." *'A gift of empty bottles? Weird.'*

She proceeded down the stairs. Instead of the big clean plastic garbage containers she was so used to, all she saw was a row of 55 gallon steel oil drums, some with lids and some not, with most being old and rusty. As she looked for one with space for her bag, she startled a cat that jumped out and scared her as well. LeeAnn loved all animals and called out "Here kitty, kitty." But the cat ran off, not even looking back. Now she clearly understood the term 'Alley Cat.' As she observed some of the overfilled garbage drums, she became instantly aware that plastic garbage bags were not invented yet, and recycling should never be mentioned. *'In a way, it is funny. They will invent a garbage bag that you can buy and then throw away, so you can buy some more garbage bags and throw them away!'*

Climbing the stairs two at time, she was greeted by her dad. "So can I see that report card?"

LeeAnn proudly retrieved it and set if before him. He reviewed it with a smile. "Wow, we had better start saving for college if you keep this up!" He reached into his wallet and produced a dollar. "Here LeeAnn, you have earned it. We are so proud of you."

LeeAnn smiled and took the dollar. "Thanks, Dad!" It was really strange, because only a day ago a dollar did not mean all that much, but in this world, she knew it meant candy, soda, and even a few shows! Maybe this world is not so bad!

Mom entered and announced. "Everyone wash their hands and get ready for dinner."

Soon they were all seated and digging into the chicken casserole. "Mom, this is delicious."

"Yes, Dear, it truly is." Her dad added.

She listened intently as her mom and dad shared the events of their day. She learned the current President was Eisenhower, and there was concern about the Russians. She had no knowledge of the nuclear threat or the cold war, but understood her parents seemed very concerned. It was conspicuous that there was no discussion about money or bills. It seemed they were so happy, yet the fact that they lived in an apartment bothered her.

"Why don't we live in a house?" She finally asked.

"We soon will. That is why your mom is working part-time at the hospital. We are saving it all and it looks like we will be looking at houses within a year or so. They are talking about building houses in the suburbs. Right now they are building an expressway, or a huge highway, so people can travel to and from the city much faster. Should that be the case, we may be looking at a brand new house in the near future." Her dad explained. "Now, they are planning them with everything included! All appliances, even a dishwasher! In fact, most of the new houses have central air conditioning and even wall to wall carpet!" He boasted.

Her mom added, "Boy, if we move to the suburbs, we will never hear the end of it. Our friends will think we abandoned them. Plus our parents will just completely flip, because they don't have any air conditioning at all."

"Where will I go to school?" LeeAnn wondered.

"Oh they have brand new schools. I guess it will also mean we must get a car." Her dad stated.

LeeAnn knew better than to say anything though she was thinking. *'We have no car?'*

"Yeah, I will miss taking the 'L' downtown." He muttered.

'I'll have to ask Papa, what's an L?'

"I agree. I like taking the bus. I will miss my bus buddies." Her mom replied.

'Mom on a bus. No way! This is one bizarre dream!' LeeAnn smiled to herself.

She sat and listened to them discuss the future and wished her sister Ashlee could witness this sight. She began to wonder; if mom and dad were really here in 1956, maybe they would still be together, as it seemed material things did not have the same value in relationships as they did in 2010. Here she could see her parents happy though living a modest life, with no quarrels about money. Even at her young age, she realized that money, credit and bills seemed a hazard of the future. As the discussion continued LeeAnn just enjoyed the moment of family warmth and togetherness. *'Papa was right, this is a priceless gift.'* There were no arguments, no cell phones ringing and no distractions from interacting as a family. She could hardly remember a time when her parents were not stressed. *'Is this really how it was?'* She wondered.

"A move to the suburbs and I get to buy my new Chevy." Dad gloated.

"It would be wonderful to get out and take a drive now and then, even if we spend two thousand." Mom replied. "Can we make it a red one?"

"Red it is. Maybe even a convertible." He suggested.

All LeeAnn could dwell on was '*Two thousand dollars for a new car?'* So she decided to satisfy a curiosity. "How much does gasoline cost?" She asked.

"That's a strange question coming from a ten year old, but gas is about 22 cents a gallon."

LeeAnn responded with a mere "Oh." In her head she was thinking '*Holy Crap! 22 cents?'*

Then came a shock, as her mom set a huge ash tray on the table and she produced a pack of cigarettes from her purse. She soon realized why the ash tray was so big, because her dad pulled out a cigar from his vest pocket. She immediately got up and started cleaning the dirty dishes from the table. '*Well Papa said almost everyone smokes.'*

"Don't bother with that, Sweetie. You go out and play. Your dad and I are going to watch the Milton Berle show in a few minutes."

'*Go out and play? Who the heck is Milton Berle?'* LeeAnn smiled. "Okay, Mom."

Her dad warned. "Be home before dark young lady!"

"Sure, Dad!" She answered. '*It's just like Papa said.*"

Leaving her parents talking and smoking at the table, she went out the front door and down the stairs to the street. There was Papa sitting on her front step, eating a hot dog.

He looked up at her, smiling, and pointed. "See that guy with a cart down the block?"

LeeAnn saw an old man with a chrome push cart with an umbrella over it. "Yes."

"He makes the best hot dogs around. No fries, but he only charges twenty cents. Man these are good."

LeeAnn was curious. "How much did you make pitching pennies?"

"I made almost forty cents. It was a pretty good day." He bragged.

"Mom and Dad were smoking!"

"LeeAnn, almost everyone smokes. Look inside one of these cars and you will find seven to eight ashtrays built in. There is one on every single door, plus large ones in the front and back for cigar smokers."

"Can I ask…What is an L?"

"It's short for 'elevated'. As in elevated train. In Chicago, we have different types of trains that people ride. When they are above ground, they are just called trains. When the trains run underground they are called subways. However, they also are on tracks that ride above the street. That's what they call the 'EL', as in elevated.

"Makes sense."

"Do you want to ride one?" He asked.

"Can I get home before dark?"

"Easy! Let's go. Since you're with me, I guess we'll pay for the ride and catch the next bus."

She was glad Papa was not going to make her jump on the back like he did. As they walked to the corner to board the bus, LeeAnn felt secure being with Papa, even though he appeared a skinny, young boy. As they boarded the bus, she watched as Papa put two nickels in a metal box, which made a ringing sound. "We're both under twelve." he told the driver. "Transfer, please." Papa requested.

LeeAnn watched as the driver took a hole-punch and made two holes in the paper transfers and handed them to Papa.

"What are those about?"

He showed her the transfer that displayed the bus line and the two holes were punched at the point of where they boarded the bus on the transfer route and the date. They were about the size of a dollar bill. "He punched the holes so we can't misuse these and board another route, or use them again tomorrow, but they allow us to transfer to another bus or train. We just show them to the next driver. With us being kids, they never check them anyway."

As they sat, LeeAnn watched as about every two blocks the bus would stop and either pick up passengers or allow them to exit. Papa was right, as the ride was smooth and quiet, since the bus was electrically powered. The driver would also yell out the name of the street at which he was stopping. When he yelled "Damen Avenue!" Papa smiled.

"Here is where we get off."

They exited the bus and entered a building, where they walked up two flights of stairs to what appeared to be a train station. "Here is where we catch the EL."

Swiftly, it arrived near silent with only the clack of the steel wheels on the track and loud screeching of the brakes. Papa showed them the transfers and soon they were riding above the street. LeeAnn was amazed. Although there was no air conditioning, the open windows provided a wonderful breeze. As they approached the Downtown area, the buildings began to get taller and taller. "Isn't this where they have the Sears Tower?" She asked.

Papa laughed. "Not for about twenty years! Right now I think the tallest building around here is the Prudential building, at about forty stories. It has an observation deck on top. If we had more time, I would take you there. If you notice, this train will travel completely around the downtown area. Someday, you may hear downtown Chicago referred to as the Loop. The reason is this elevated train travels a circle and heads back to its point of origin; therefore, it's a loop."

"Did you know all of this at ten years old?"

"Yes, most of it. Whenever I lived with my dad, I was, at most times, on my own. My dad was always moving from place to place. When he was not living with my mom, we more or less lived out of a suitcase. We never had furniture, or anything, and it seemed I was always enrolling in new schools. Little by little, I learned the whole north side of the city by heart."

LeeAnn was staring out the window. In the distance, she could see Lake Michigan, which looked like an ocean, as the water seemed to meet the horizon.

"I met a nice woman that lives right next to us. It was weird."

"What was so weird?" Papa asked.

"She tried to give me some empty bottles."

Papa immediately got excited. "Can you still get them?"

"Uh, yeah, I think so."

"Cool! How many were there?"

LeeAnn just guessed. "Well, there was a whole section of her porch, so maybe twenty. Why, they are just empty bottles?"

"It's a treasure! Each one is worth a nickel. I assume they are quarts?"

"Yeah, big bottles."

Papa smiled, "Looks like we'll have some money for tomorrow! So, how do you like the ride?"

"This is like a theme park!" LeeAnn was very aware that people were boarding and exiting. Some were dressed in what she considered 'dress' clothes for the office, and others looked a bit casual and even a bit rougher, yet no one bothered them but to smile. She found herself studying their shoes, as everyone had leather shoes. She also took notice that the people were of all colors and ethnicities.

"I have never seen so many different types of people."

"Chicago is what is called a melting pot, because almost every country is represented here. There is China Town, Italian Taylor Street, German Town, Greek Town, Polish, Lithuanian, Jewish, Black and various Spanish speaking groups, all in one city." Papa explained.

"This is a lot different than Missouri." LeeAnn replied.

LeeAnn sat back and just watched the city go by, as the train rounded the loop and was returning in the direction from which they came. She clearly understood the feeling of freedom that Papa had spoken of so many times. What she initially thought was a whopper of a tale, now seemed like the absolute truth, and her heart pounded with excitement. '*Here I am at ten years old and I can't even go to the store by myself.*' This thought sparked a question.

"Papa, if you were ten years old in 2010, would you be able to do this same thing?"

"No way! I don't think anything that I did could be done without risking one's life. In one week of 2010, Chicago had 38 shootings in just one weekend. They now have the National Guard patrolling with police. Sadly, this way of life is long gone."

For an instant, she, too, became sad. She knew this was only going to be a brief trip in this secure world of long ago. "Papa, when I go to sleep tonight, is this dream over?"

"Nah, I still think you have lots to see."

LeeAnn smiled. "Great! What will we do next?"

"Whatever we like! I can take you to meet your great grandma and even your great, great grandma!"

LeeAnn watched as the train became full, but when a woman stepped on and there were no seats, she saw at least three men stand and offer their seat to her. *'Strange'*

"Papa, why did a bunch of men stand and offer their seats to that woman?"

"Because, that is what we once called chivalry. During this point in time, a man would always offer a woman his seat. It is literally impossible for a woman to be standing while any man is seated. Plus, if a man is near, a woman will always have a door opened for her. There are so many things that we have dropped from what was once considered proper etiquette. In 1956, on dates, a woman never pays and a man can never lay a hand on a woman. They won't even show anything like that in movies. There is no such thing as a woman that needs to know self defense. All she has to do is let out a scream and ten men will come running. Spousal abuse is just not an issue. Someday, when you are a bit older, I will explain how women in our society became so degraded. But, not today!"

As LeeAnn watched, it was exactly as Papa said. Regardless of how pretty or how old, when a woman got on the train, a number of men would offer her their seats. This really struck a nerve, because LeeAnn was learning martial arts for self defense in 2010. She was learning that a woman must even protect herself when dating. Soon she heard the conductor announce "Daaaaamen Avenue!"

"Did you notice how he made the announcement?"

"Yeah, a little strange!"

"Many conductors take great pride in the unique way they announce their stops. Some even sing them out."

"No way!" LeeAnn studied Papa's face, but she could tell by his expression it was the truth.

"Yeah way! Here is where we get off."

It wasn't like Disneyland, but this ride was fun, and the time seemed to just fly by. Through the station they traveled down two flights to the street, where a number of buses were waiting. They quickly boarded.

"See? You wondered how I got around. I'll bet you could make this trip again on your own if you wanted. All you need is a good memory for a few street names, or to remember some key landmarks. Traveling the city is fun."

"I would still be afraid." LeeAnn replied.

"That is the sad difference in times and I guess you have good reason. You see, I had nothing to be afraid of as I was never exposed to the same realities that you are conditioned to. My life was exactly the opposite. I was always more afraid of coming home to a drunken father, than being on the street. We do have a legal curfew and no children are supposed to be on the street without an adult after 10 P.M., so more than once a policeman has walked me home."

"You're kidding?"

"No, Officer Finn knows me well." Papa laughed.

"What do you do so late at night?"

"Just hang around on the corner with the big kids. Let's go, our stop is coming up. You know better than to mention this trip to your parents, right? They might go berserk. Just so you know, the standard answer for the question 'Where were you?' is 'At the park.' This is one answer that is never questioned."

Papa and LeeAnn exited the bus and walked the block to LeeAnn's apartment. "Well, I guess that's it for today. Sleep late and whenever you are ready, just come outside and I'll find you."

"What are you going to do?" LeeAnn was concerned, for she realized that her Papa had no one to go home to, or his father may be drunk and hit him.

"Ah, don't worry about me. Remember how old I really am, so we both know I will survive. I've got a few people to see and then I'll go home and read a book. At this point in my life, I love reading Frank Buck and his adventures in the jungles."

"Guess I'll see you tomorrow?"

"Yes, for sure."

LeeAnn skipped up the stairs and when she entered, her mom and dad were watching television. "Hi!"

Mom studied her face. "You look a little red in the face. Are you feeling okay?"

LeeAnn smiled. "Mom, I feel fine."

"Come here, let me feel your forehead and see if you have a fever."

Mom felt her forehead. "You do feel a little flushed. Maybe I should call Doctor Lassen and have him stop by and take a look at you."

"At the house?" LeeAnn asked in shock.

"What is so unusual about that, young lady?"

"Uh, nothing, but I feel fine mom. I really do!" Meanwhile she was thinking, *'Will a doctor actually come to your house? Holy crap, this is a much different world.'*

"Hon, she knows when she is ill. Come sit with us." Her dad beckoned. "They announced today that they have successfully invented the ability to broadcast television in color. Imagine, someday we will be able to watch color TV!"

LeeAnn managed to fake some slight excitement. "Wow, that would really be something. How soon will we get one?" Inside she was laughing when thinking '*Yeah it will be in color and as big as the whole wall!'*

"Oh, it will be years before we can buy one in the stores and I'm sure they will be really expensive."

"I went to the record store with Joyce and heard the new record by Elvis!" LeeAnn announced. Her dad laughed.

"Yeah, Elvis the pelvis!" He grinned. "He moves around like his pants are on fire. A Perry Como he is not."

'*Who the heck is Perry Como?'* LeeAnn wondered.

"That Rock and Roll is being played more and more often on radio." Mom replied.

"I don't care, nothing can beat Patty Page, or Sinatra, or Bing." Dad responded with authority. "Rock and Roll is just a phase. In a year, they won't remember what an Elvis is!"

"I don't know, that program 'Bandstand' is really becoming popular, especially since that new announcer took over." Mom stated.

"What is so special about him? Does he jump around too?"

"His name is Dick Clark, and he looks like a teenager himself."

"Ah, I'll take the 'Hit Parade' any day! They know the kind of music people really like."

'*Oh my God, are you in for a surprise!'* LeeAnn thought. *'Boy it would be fun to tell them a bit about the future. Wait till they see Katie Perry or Lady Gaga!'* She noticed that although her dad had his shoes off and tie loosened, to her it looked very uncomfortable.

"Dad, do you ever just chill?" No sooner than she said it, LeeAnn knew she made a huge verbal mistake.

"Chill? Chill? What the heck does that mean, young lady?"

"I mean relax. You look uncomfortable with your tie on." She explained.

"LeeAnn, why didn't you just say that? Chill? Is that some kind of slang they are spreading at school? Don't be picking up any of that slang, especially since we are paying good money for tuition so you can learn proper English. Chill? What the heck is that?"

'Geez wait until they find out what's coming if they think the word 'chill' is a problem!'

"Sorry, Dad." LeeAnn offered.

"Well, to answer your question, I want to look proper if someone stops by. What would I do, answer the door in my pajamas?" He laughed.

"No, I just meant maybe you would be more comfortable wearing something casual." LeeAnn explained.

"Yeah, that would make your mom real happy." He replied sarcastically. "I could put on clean clothes just to sit around in. Imagine the pile of clothes she would have to wash and iron. We're lucky enough to have a laundry on the block."

LeeAnn was now surprised that they had no washer and dryer. This never occurred to her. "Yeah, you're right Dad. I wasn't thinking."

LeeAnn was curious as how her father in this day and age might look toward the future. "Dad, do you ever think we will travel to the moon?"

Her dad looked at her curiously. "Are you reading Jules Verne?"

"Who is Jules Verne?" LeeAnn asked.

"He was the author of 'From the Earth to the Moon', a very popular novel.

"Uh, no. I just wondered."

"Well there is talk of Russia launching what is called a 'satellite' next year, but I think it's all just talk. A satellite is a capsule that will float in space and circle the globe. Our only worry is that they might put a bomb in it. Why would we want to go to the moon? It's not like Wyoming and Montana are overpopulated." He laughed. "Right now, what I am hoping for is jet planes. Imagine being able to fly to California in a few hours? Now that would be progress!"

'No jet airplanes? I am afraid to ask how long it takes to get there now!'

"Well, I'm going on to bed." LeeAnn sighed. Actually, she was afraid to talk about anything, as she did not really know what she could safely discuss.

"Kind of early, isn't it? You know you can sleep as late as you like. I must be at work at nine, but I will leave a bowl of cereal out for you if you get up late." Mom stated.

"Can I just go out?" LeeAnn wondered.

"LeeAnn, you know the rules. You stay in the neighborhood. I should be home a little after lunchtime."

LeeAnn smiled. *'Papa was right! It's like being free!'*

As she kissed them each goodnight, her dad reminded her. "Don't spend that dollar all in one place!" What would normally sound like a remark that was absurd, suddenly made a lot of sense. "And, you be careful crossing those busy streets!" He added.

She brushed her teeth and washed up, and went to bed hoping she would fall asleep quickly, for she knew the next day would bring nothing but adventures. As her eyes became heavy, she pondered the thought. *'What if I dream? What do you dream about if you are already in a dream?'* As she pondered that puzzle, she fell fast asleep.

She awoke early and anxious to face the new day. Her mom had not left for work yet, and as she wandered to the bathroom, she cheerfully said "Good morning, Mom!"

Her mom was surprised. "Being the first day of your summer vacation, I expected you to sleep until noon."

"No, for some reason, I awoke early."

"Well, dear, your cereal is waiting."

After brushing and washing, she went back to her room. She noticed her clothes were gone and had likely picked up by her mom as being dirty. She went to her closet and on a shelf she saw a few pairs of jeans. Grabbing one, they looked washed out. One pair even had a hole in the knee. *'Cool!'* She put them on and picked a top and proceeded to the kitchen table.

Her mom was staring at her with a stern look on her face.

"What?" LeeAnn asked.

"Young lady, you are not going out in those jeans! You look like an orphan, for God's sake. In case you didn't notice, they have a hole in them!"

LeeAnn did not understand. "So?"

"So? What will people think if you walk around looking like that? I put those on the shelf to give to the Salvation Army. You go put on a decent pair, right now."

Again LeeAnn forgot herself and mumbled "Whatever."

"Whatever? Whatever? What the heck does that mean? You mean 'Yes, Mother."

"Yes, Mom…sorry."

"LeeAnn, what is with this abbreviated manner of speaking? Don't you mean to say 'I'm sorry'? Whatever? Sorry? And last night, chill? I don't care how you talk to your friends, but you speak properly to adults. Complete sentences please! That is how the Neanderthals talked, all in one and two word sentences!" Her mom began to mimic cavemen. "Food, good!" mom grunted. "Me go work." She growled. "Chill!" She laughed. "You have to admit, I sound like a cavewomen!"

LeeAnn laughed loudly, for in a way, her mom was correct. All the modern abbreviated speech was really a throw back to early mankind, when they had a severe lack of vocabulary.

"Yes, Mother." She answered properly, then added a grunting. "Cereal Good! Me Happy!"

They both began sharing an infectiously hilarious moment.

Going to her room and changing, she didn't understand why her mom didn't realize the washed out denim was so much more comfortable than the stiff jeans she had to choose from? Returning to the table, she made another blunder. "Maybe, you can cut the legs down and I can make shorts out of them?" LeeAnn suggested.

"What is going through your head young lady? Who ever heard of such a thing? You have some shorts in your drawer. Is this a new philosophy you have come up with? Maybe if you put a hole in your sleeve, I'll just cut if off!" Again, they began laughing.

LeeAnn ate her breakfast as her mom walked about mumbling. "Cut off the legs of those old worn out jeans. We can't just chop up our clothes. The neighbors will think we are some kind of Gypsies." Her mom kissed her on her head while saying goodbye and left for work.

"Man, I guess that idea is way before its time." LeeAnn said to herself, once she was alone.

As she sat eating her breakfast and wondering how she would meet up with Papa, off in the distance she could hear a sound that she only knew from Papa's stories. It was the loud clanging of a bell, and a deep baritone voice of a man loudly singing.

"Come and get them! POTATOES! TOMATOES!"

As she listened, she could hear the sound was getting closer and closer. She knew she had to see this! LeeAnn quickly arose from the table and went to empty the unfinished bowl of cereal in the sink. Only then did she realize that there was no garbage disposal. So she drained the milk into the sink and scraped the leftover cereal into the garbage bag. She already knew that there was no air conditioning, but realized that their apartment was left with the windows wide open and with only the screens to keep the bugs out. The kitchen door was open and only a screen door was closed, but unlocked, as only a small hook could keep it from being opened. *'I guess they don't worry about crime as much during these years?'*

She ran out the back door and down the back stairs to the alley. She could see the horse drawn wagon slowly moving in her direction. The clanging of the bell became louder, as did the sound of the vendor's booming voice. "POTATOES! TOMATOES!" She watched as he stopped, and the women hurried out to pick their produce off his wagon. The man quickly weighed it on his old fashioned hanging scale, and they exchanged money. She noticed that most of the woman brought their own cloth shopping bags. As he moved closer, she could hear the clear sound of the horse's hooves, and the clop, clop, clop, clop was clear and distinct. LeeAnn knew about horses and was a good rider, so this clop sound told her that this horse was likely wearing good shoes, considering it was walking on concrete.

As she waited for the wagon to reach her alley, she realized that Papa was standing beside her. "You always thought I was kidding, didn't you?"

"Yes, I always thought it was a bit of a tale." She grinned.

"I don't think you will like what you see."

"Why?"

"You'll see."

When the wagon came close and as the vegetable man was yelling and ringing the bell, she could now realize what Papa was referring to. It was the first time she had ever seen a horse wear 'blinders.' This head gear blocked the horse's peripheral vision so it could only see directly ahead. The horse appeared to be an older one, as LeeAnn could judge because of the general appearance and the pockets above the eyes. It was overweight, un-groomed and pulling a large heavy wagon. The wheels on the wagon were huge, like those of an old western covered wagon, but it was made oversized with heavy modern day lumber and added to that were hundreds of pounds of fruit and vegetables. *'This poor old girl.'* She thought. This horse's total day was spent pulling the wagon about a hundred feet and stopping, over and over, all day long, from morning to night.

As the women came out and were picking their fruit and vegetables, she looked toward Papa and said softly. "This makes me sad. She needs some real exercise and good grooming."

"You can see by the feed bag and bucket of water that this horse is well fed and as far as I can judge, for an old horse, at least it's a life."

"Think I can give her a treat?" LeeAnn asked.

"Go ahead and pet her. I'll be right back."

She watched as Papa went up to the man and boldly asked. "Sir, can I get an apple?"

The man who had an Italian accent replied. "Go on sonny, you take-a what-a you like."

LeeAnn watched as Papa thanked him and picked a huge delicious apple. With the man tending to his customers in the back of the cart, Papa returned to the front where LeeAnn was stroking the horse's head. "Here." He tossed her the apple.

Since the apple was very big, she looked to Papa for help. "Can you split this in half?"

"Sure." Papa pulled out a good sized pocket knife and cut the apple in quarters. "Here you go."

She fed the horse a piece at a time, and the horse tossed her head in enjoyment. LeeAnn smiled, and could tell from the horse's teeth that at least her diet was a good one. She then realized that Papa carried a pretty big knife.

"If no one ever bothers you, why do you carry that knife?"

He took it from his pocket and gave her a closer look. "This isn't just a knife. This is also my can opener, fork, spoon, and screw driver." She watched as he folded out each element. "I can go into a store, buy a can of beans, or fruit, open it and eat it, or I could have peeled that apple. With this, I can fix my bike, or pry open a door or window if my dad locks me out by accident. This is life saver. It's called a camping knife."

"I just saw the knife part and it is rather large. Is it legal for you to have that?"

"Legal?" Papa laughed. "I guess we are going to have to visit the department store and I'll show you what kids our age can buy right off the shelf. You will really get a kick out of that! They give away pocket knives to kids at some stores. They put their name on them and consider it good advertizing."

Just as they were talking, the horse began to poop. As she did, the vegetable man brought a huge bucket that was hanging on the side of the wagon and quickly took a small shovel and cleaned it up.

Papa smiled. "I guess you can answer Ashlee's question now. In fact, he will likely sell the bucket when full to someone with a garden, as manure is the best fertilizer. Maybe that's why the horse is so well fed!" They both laughed.

Having satisfied her curiosity about the vegetable cart, LeeAnn was ready for a new adventure. "What will we do next?"

"Let me show you the park, and then we'll be off to see some stores."

They walked from the alley and down the street. As they walked, LeeAnn noticed everything. As they passed the back yards, she could see waves of clothes hanging on clotheslines. "Does no one have a dryer?" She wondered.

"Well, if I have a chance, I will show you the most common washing machine. It has a large tub for washing and rinsing, and has what is called a 'wringer'. It literally crushes the clothes on rollers and squeezes the water out of them. Clotheslines are very common. In the winter, the clothes are hung in the basements or on racks that they call clothes horses. Dryers are available, but considered too expensive, as they are not as efficient as what you are used to. Oh yeah, everything must be ironed as there is no such thing as wash and wear clothes."

"You're kidding?"

"You've never seen a big ironing board?"

"No, but I have seen an iron. Mom uses the counter top, but not very often."

As they reached the park, to LeeAnn, it seemed enormous. It had all the things her school had. There were swings and monkey bars, but also tennis courts and a beautiful baseball diamond with bleachers, plus a volley ball court and a tetherball. On the opposite side was another baseball diamond that was not so elaborate. "Why are there two baseball diamonds, and why are they so different?"

"One is for little league and the other one is for softball."

LeeAnn noticed a green building off to the side. "What's that, Papa?"

"It's the park district building. It has washrooms, and you can get some equipment there, like a basketball or whatever."

LeeAnn laughed. "You just goofed. You said whatever!"

Papa smiled. "Boy, you are right. There are no whatever's in 1956."

"This park is really nice."

"Actually, it isn't that great. Some have swimming pools and even football fields. There is one a few miles from here that has an Olympic pool and a high dive! Chicago has some great parks! Humboldt Park even has boats you can rent!"

"Boats? At a park? How big is it?"

"Huge. It would be measured in square miles. Let's just say bigger than Silver Dollar City."

"Wow!" LeeAnn gasped, knowing Papa was not kidding.

They approached a huge, round, concrete fountain with three spigots pumping water continuously twelve inches in the air. Papa bent over and took a long drink. "Man, that's cold!"

"Papa, this drinking fountain is huge! Does it run all the time?"

"All spring, summer and fall, but not winter."

"Do all parks have these?"

"All that I have seen."

"Isn't this wasteful?" LeeAnn wondered.

"Sure is, but it's not something we considered in 1956."

She watched as Papa washed off his knife. "Well, what's next?"

"Have you ever heard of Buster Brown?" He asked with a smile, knowing LeeAnn would draw a blank.

"Buster who?"

"Come on, let's go have some fun!"

Chapter Four

THIS WAS A STRANGE NEW experience for LeeAnn, just being out on her own with no adults and no predetermined schedule. There she was, with her Papa, alone in the strange, big city. LeeAnn followed along, as it seemed Papa knew exactly where he was going. It was only a few short blocks before they came upon a very busy street. The sign read 'North Ave.' The first thing she observed was an elaborate theater across the street. It had a huge sign that was over two stories tall, proudly flaunting the name "Tiffin Theater." Surrounding it was a massive marquee displaying "The Searchers", starring John Wayne.

"Your theaters look a lot different than ours. Look at all the lights!"

"Well, just going to the show was a big deal. The movies actually stayed the same for a much longer period of time. This movie may be here for a month or more. There was no such thing as a new movie being released every week. Come on, let's cross over...See the display windows under the marquee?" Papa asked.

They both looked at all the pictures and posters. The pictures showed scenes from the movie that was currently showing, while others displayed previews of coming attractions.

"This is the only way to find out what new movies are being released, other than reading magazines. There are no commercials on TV for movies. Those scene photos actually travel with the film from city to city. These major movies are shown in the big cities first, and then travel to smaller towns. People in Springfield might not see this movie until six months from now."

"You mean, everyone can't see the same movie all at once across the country?"

"Nope. See the scene photos? Those are called 'lobby cards', because they are shown in the lobby. I have a huge vintage collection in 2010."

"Can I see them?" LeeAnn asked.

"Sure, when we return. Do you want to hear something really

unbelievable? Once this movie leaves the theaters, it cannot be seen ever again; unless, maybe they show it on TV five to ten years from now."

"You're kidding." LeeAnn gasped. "You mean, if you don't go to the show, you missed it completely?"

"Absolutely! This is why I can't understand why people pay so much to go to the theater in 2010, when the movies come out on DVD within weeks. Plus, during this time, people had proper etiquette. Everyone sat quietly and no one talked. Today, people talk and cell phones ring... theater-going isn't as enjoyable."

"You're joking!"

"No, I'm not. We have no DVDs or video tapes. The movie itself is on film, and there is no way of recording and duplicating it."

"I guess we're pretty lucky in 2010."

"I'll say!"

LeeAnn stood, enjoying the smell of fresh popcorn. She noticed a store across the street with the sign that read 'Buster Brown Shoes.'

"Papa, what's so special about Buster Brown?"

"Come on; I'll show you."

They crossed the street and together they entered the store. Immediately, LeeAnn noticed a new, foreign scent. It was the smell of hundreds of pairs of leather shoes. She followed Papa to the counter, where he picked up what looked like a comic book. "They're free!" He told her. So LeeAnn grabbed a copy, which read "The Adventures of Buster Brown."

"I come here and get a copy every month." Papa stated.

"I guess comics are more popular than in 2010?"

"Very much so. Even the Catholic school has a monthly comic called 'Treasure Chest.' This comic teaches religion and history. In this era, comics can be very educational. There is a comic called 'Classics Illustrated.' Basically, these are all comic versions of many major literary works. Many kids are like me, in that if they read the comic and enjoy the story, they will go to library and read the whole book."

LeeAnn remembered what her dad had asked at dinner the previous night. "Would they have 'From the Earth to the Moon', by Jules Verne?"

"Sure! I have read that one myself. Jules Verne also wrote 'Journey to the Center of the Earth'. Those are great books. The greatest was the movie version of Jules Verne's, '20,000 Leagues under the Sea', by Walt Disney. Get the book. You'll love it, and if you like Jules Verne, you will love H.G. Wells and his book, 'The Time Machine'."

"Papa, did you know all this when you were ten?"

"**When I was your age,** I knew all that and a lot more. You see, everything was educational. Whether it was comics or movies, you were always learning. Have you ever heard of the Alamo?"

"Alamo? What's that?"

"Well, today it's more or less a shrine in San Antonio, Texas, but the battle of the Alamo was a pivotal battle between the Americans and Mexicans over what is now the state of Texas. Because we lost that battle and Americans died while fighting bravely although vastly outnumbered, 'Remember the Alamo' became the battle cry for the rest of the war. Because of such, Texas eventually became a state. Do you know of Custer's last stand?"

"Uh, No. Custard?" LeeAnn replied.

"No, Custer. It is where General George Armstrong Custer took his army to fight what he thought was a single tribe of Indians, and instead, met up with an army of Indians that had gathered and combined from many tribes. He was totally outnumbered and he was wiped out. That is why they called it his 'last stand'."

"I have never heard of any of this."

"**When I was your age,** I was exposed to volumes of history through movies. I knew of the Great Depression, Civil war, slavery, pirates, medieval times, prohibition, World War II, and lots about Indians, or Native Americans. At age ten, I could name at least ten or twelve tribes and knew where they lived geographically, all from just movies. Probably the single largest difference is that movies never promoted bad or illegal behavior. Unless the movie was historical, usually the good guy always won. And comics? Forget it. Classic comics were a tour through literary history. You could pick up a comic and get Robinson Crusoe, A Midsummer Night's Dream, or over a hundred-fifty book and historical titles, for without having 300 television channels and DVD's, reading was our only enjoyment. **When I was your age,** just growing up was a continuous education."

As they talked, they never noticed Joyce coming up from behind. "Hi, LeeAnn!" She said happily. This was followed by a serious "Hello Ed Burk."

"Uh, hi Joyce. We just ran into each other after getting a Buster Brown comic." LeeAnn explained.

"LeeAnn, what are you up to?"

LeeAnn wasn't sure how to respond, but decided to basically tell the truth. "Well, Ed and I were going to a department store to see some of the new toys."

Although running around with a boy seemed unusual, Joyce decided it sounded like fun. "Are you going to Abrams?"

Papa decided to dominate the conversation. "Yeah, I wanted to see the new Davey Crockett toys."

Joyce asked politely. "May I go along?"

LeeAnn found herself skipping through this pleasant dream. There they were, three ten year olds, alone and exploring the world. She clearly understood why her Papa mourned the loss of his past. Abrams was a rather small department store, as far as LeeAnn was concerned. It was nowhere near the size of the stores that she was so used to. It only had one small floor, but also had departments in the basement, which is where the toy department was. Being conditioned to a toy store that is gigantic, the toy department seemed sparse, to say the least. Knowing Joyce was with them, she would withhold her comments until later when she and Papa could talk freely. Fortunately, Joyce decided she wanted to look at the new dresses. "Do you mind?" She asked. LeeAnn was relieved, as now she could talk to Papa freely.

"Here, let's check out some lethal weapons!" Papa suggested. "This is a 'spud gun.' You jam the sharp barrel into a potato and shoot a potato pellet."

"You're kidding?"

"This is nothing. Look at the latest BB rifle."

"Kids can buy BB guns?"

"Sure. Check this out." Papa picked up a heavy duty sling shot. "Put a marble in this and you can really do some damage."

"Oh my Gosh!" LeeAnn gasped.

"Here." Papa pointed out. "Check out this chemistry set. There are maybe fifty bottles of chemicals. Not only are some of these poison, but some are dangerous carcinogens. Not to mention you can create lethal gasses and even a fire or an explosion."

"You can buy these at your age?"

"Yeah, all these and more! Ah, here is one of my favorites." Papa picked up a bow and arrow. "You just pull the suction cups off the tips of the arrows and bingo! It's capable of killing someone. Then, we also have darts."

LeeAnn examined a dart board containing eight sharp metal darts. "Papa, these could really hurt someone."

"Oh yes, and a lot of kids got hurt with these. LeeAnn, I could go on forever, but let me show you just a few more of my favorites." Papa went to an electric train set and opened the cover. "See, this is electric. This transformer has two terminals on top where you hook up the electricity. See that wire? You hook up the two wires to the terminals and plug it into the wall. Guess what happens if you plug it into the wall and then handle the terminals? You possibly get 115 volts and electrocuted. Or, even if you do it correctly and merely set your hand on top of the transformer, touching both terminals which also could be deadly. I won't even show you wood burners. That is a great toy! It is a tool the heats up to 800 degrees, and you burn drawings into wood. The problem, is if you accidently touch the tip, you get a third degree burn; or, if you forget and leave it plugged in, it could become an instant house fire."

"Papa, how did you survive?"

"Oh, I had my share of injuries and burns, but I was just lucky, I guess. I did know a boy that lost his eye. I knew quite a few that got stabbed. Here, check out the knives."

As LeeAnn gazed at the selection, she asked. "You can buy any of these?"

"Where do you think I got my camping knife?"

"Geez, it's a wonder any boys survived." LeeAnn responded.

"Oh, the girls were not safe from injury either. They had real miniature electric irons, and an electric oven. Plus, play silverware sets made up of thin, sharp tin knives and forks, not to mention sewing sets with tons of needles and a pair of sharp scissors. In fact, there is a miniature electric sewing machine that will let you sew your fingers together!" He joked. "You don't even want to see what is available for infants to swallow and choke on."

"Look Papa, Winky Dink!" LeeAnn laughed.

"Yeah, that's the famous Winky Dink set that hardly anyone bought."

Joyce came running over. "LeeAnn, you have to see these new sweaters!"

LeeAnn looked toward Papa. He smiled. "You go, I'll hang around outside."

LeeAnn and Joyce made a beeline for the clothes department. Papa just stood and watched. Though he appeared a skinny ten year old, he was seeing his granddaughter through 65 year old eyes, and she was exploring this new world and having the time of her life. As his eyes became a bit misty, he found his way out to the street. Meanwhile, LeeAnn and Joyce were plowing through fashions.

"Look at these sweaters LeeAnn! They are beautiful!"

LeeAnn agreed, but did not like the available colors. "I don't like all the colors."

The colors of the era were primarily pastels, with nothing being very bright and bold.

"What color are you looking for?" Joyce wondered.

"Orange. Maybe yellow or red."

"Orange? They don't make anything in orange?"

"Maybe they should. I think kids might like brighter colors."

"I just think the softer colors are so pretty."

LeeAnn took notice that whole department for her age group consisted of a small wall of shelves, a few table displays, and a few racks. This was nowhere near to the mammoth selection she had in 2010. She found it obvious that there were no designer names. The strangest item was advertized as 'gym' shoes, as they were the same 'old school' design that was popular in 2010. '*Weird!*'

Just then, Papa found them. "Come on outside! It's Little Oscar!"

"Oh, let's go!" Joyce squealed.

'*What the heck is a little Oscar?*' LeeAnn wondered as she followed along.

When they got outside, just parked down the block was a huge vehicle shaped like a giant hot dog in a bun! It had the Oscar Meyer logo on the side. Out of a hatch on the roof was a midget in a chef's hat, waving at all the children! In the meantime, through a serving window at street level, they passed out free hot dogs and a little whistle shaped like an Oscar Meyer hot dog.

'*I can't believe this!*' LeeAnn thought. "Does he just drive around all over?"

"Yeah! You never know where Little Oscar will show up. I guess we are just lucky!" Joyce exclaimed.

"That's called 'Little Oscar's Wiener mobile'." Papa laughed.

As they enjoyed their hot dogs, Papa explained. "Oscar Meyer started here in Chicago. Many other companies are from Chicago, as well. Dad's root beer, Mars Candy Company, and many others are located here."

"Don't forget Fannie May Candies!" Joyce added.

"I love Vienna hot dogs." Papa stated.

"SSHHH! Don't let Little Oscar hear you!" Joyce warned.

"Well, these are the best you can bring home, because Vienna is only available at hot dog stands. Hey, I don't care if that little midget hears me."

"Ed Burk, no wonder Sister Bernice was always whacking you with her ruler. Do you just have a habit of saying what's on your mind?" Joyce scolded.

"I guess?" Papa replied.

LeeAnn laughed, because so many times she had heard her Nana tell Papa the exact same thing. She knew Papa never minced words, and was known for being direct, candid, and concise in his communication. '*So I guess Papa was always like that.*' She thought.

LeeAnn ate her hot dog and just absorbed all the sights. It really was like being in a theme park. Across the street was a theater with an enormous lit marquee like she had never seen before. As they talked, the electric buses breezed by and people swarmed the street going from shop to shop, gathering their wants and needs. Right in front of her was a hot dog the size of a bus, with a midget wearing a chef's hat, waving to everyone. It all seemed surreal. She really began to understand why her Papa was so unhappy with world of 2010. Most of all, it seemed everywhere they traveled was safe, and never did they consider being threatened.

"Want to go to the 5 & 10 cent store? They have a soda fountain and I'll treat." Papa suggested.

'*5 & 10 cent store?*' LeeAnn wondered. '*It must be like a dollar store?*'

"Come on, Woolworth's is just down the block."

So the three adventurers made their way down the block to a store that had a sign that stated 'Woolworth's 5 & 10.' Inside, were long isles of display tables with everything from toys to cosmetics. As LeeAnn looked around, she saw brooms and mops, cloth for making clothes, candy, and even hardware. In the rear was sandwich counter with a lit menu of sandwiches and ice cream creations. '*Cool!*' She thought.

"Can we get three cokes?" Papa asked, as he laid a quarter on the counter.

LeeAnn noticed that the man gave Papa a dime in change. It occurred to her that there seemed to be no tax? "Nickel cokes and no sales tax?"

"Sure, sales tax is two percent, or two cents on every dollar. So you pay no tax on anything priced under fifty cents."

LeeAnn noticed that the dime looked different than what she was used to seeing. She made a mental note to ask Papa about the coins. As they enjoyed their cokes, Joyce was curious about where LeeAnn had moved from.

"Was Missouri that much different?" Joyce questioned.

"Very different." LeeAnn answered while smiling at Papa.

"How so?" Joyce wondered.

LeeAnn had to think fast and answer in terms that would make sense to Joyce.

"Well, for one thing, we don't have the little stores like Chicago has. We have to travel to get to the shopping area."

"So you could not just walk to the corner and get ice cream or anything?"

"No, my parents must drive me."

"Wow. So you did not run any errands for your parents, like getting some milk or a newspaper and such?" Joyce asked.

"Uh no, everything was farther away." LeeAnn offered as an explanation.

"Like living in farm country?"

"Uh, yeah!" LeeAnn realized that this was the easiest explanation.

"Did you ever ride a horse?" Joyce asked.

"I used to ride all the time."

"Really?"

"Oh, we all ride, even my mom and dad and little sister." As soon as she uttered the words, LeeAnn knew she may have made a mistake.

"You have a sister?"

"Yeah, Ashlee. She is a few years younger."

Instead of any uncomfortable further questions, Joyce only said "You're lucky. I wish I had a sister."

"Yeah, my sister is pretty cool most of the time." LeeAnn replied.

"I always wondered about that. Does your sister ever mess with your stuff?"

"All the time, but you get used to it, as that's what little sisters do."

"Does she look like you?" Joyce asked.

LeeAnn thought that she would have a little fun. "No, she looks a lot different. She is tall and has black hair and can be very mean at times. She really has an attitude problem."

"Really?"

"Yeah, that's why I didn't bring her along. Plus, she uses swears all the time."

"She swears? What do your parents do?" Joyce wondered.

"They are always washing her mouth out with soap."

Papa began to laugh at LeeAnn's fabricated description, and walked away, as if interested in something he saw.

LeeAnn continued. "I hate when she throws her screaming fits when she doesn't get her way."

"Fits?"

"Oh, yeah. She screams and throws things. At times, even my parents run from her."

Joyce became serious. "Maybe I *am* glad I don't have a sister..."

"Yeah, sometimes I wonder if the hospital made a mistake and we brought home the wrong baby. That can happen, you know."

Papa listened from a distance, and was laughing hysterically. It seemed LeeAnn had inherited his story telling skills. *'By the time she is done, poor Joyce will be afraid to meet Ashlee!'*

As they sipped their cokes, LeeAnn realized that instead of being afraid to talk, she could have some fun and leave Joyce some thoughts to remember her by.

"Joyce, do you think that rock and roll will become so popular that it will have its own radio channels?"

"You mean channels? Like more than one? I don't think so."

"Why?"

"The older people don't really like the music very much."

"I'll bet rock and roll takes over the whole radio." LeeAnn predicted.

"You think?"

"In fact, I'll bet they will be able to put twenty songs on a record some day."

Joyce just laughed. "I don't think so. That would be one huge record! How big would that record player be?"

"It will fit in my hand." LeeAnn held out her palm.

"That's crazy! Now you're being silly."

"Well, imagine if you could. Wouldn't that be cool?"

"Yeah, but impossible. As long as you are dreaming, why stop there?" Joyce challenged.

"Okay, what if you could have a telephone that you could carry along with you?" LeeAnn replied.

Joyce just laughed. "That would have to be one long cord! No way!"

Papa returned and added to the imaginary device. "As long as you're dreaming, why not have one that you can watch TV on, or even see movies? Who knows?"

"All in your hand? Ed Burk, you're crazy." Joyce laughed.

"Yeah, you're right, especially since my dad doesn't even have a phone."

"Well, we have a phone, but other people talk on it sometimes." LeeAnn replied.

"LeeAnn, what do you want to be when you grow up? I want to be a nurse."

"Like a nurse or an EMT?"

"What's an EMT?" Joyce wondered.

"Like a paramedic."

"What's a paramedic?"

"Uh, they work with the fire department."

"They do? I never heard of that. The fire department is just firemen."

"Who do you think comes in an emergency when you call 911?"

It was at that moment that LeeAnn could see Papa shaking his head 'no!' She knew she had made a giant mistake.

"What is 911?" Joyce asked.

LeeAnn had to think quick. "Oh, in Missouri, it is like dialing the operator. I forgot, you don't have that here." She thought to herself '*Duh, there is no 911. In fact, there are no EMTs or paramedics in 1956!*'

"What do you want to be?" Joyce asked, and LeeAnn would soon find herself in trouble again.

"I would like to join the police force." LeeAnn replied without hesitation.

"You're kidding, right?"

"Why would I be kidding?" LeeAnn wondered.

"Why? Simply because women can't join the police force."

"They can't?" LeeAnn gasped.

"No. Have you ever seen a woman in a police uniform? I don't think so."

"Well, someday they will, and when that day comes, I will join." LeeAnn knew she had made a mistake, not realizing women could never be police officers in 1956.

"Well, I have to get home and do my chores or my mom will get upset." Joyce stated, pushing aside her empty coke glass.

"Let us walk you." LeeAnn offered.

They left the Woolworth's Dime store and made their way along the busy street. As they passed a small grocery store, Papa stated "That's where I make a little money."

"Do you work there?" Joyce asked.

"No. All I do is hang around outside waiting for a kind looking lady that has a lot of bags to carry, and offer to help her carry them home. They will always give you at least a quarter."

"That's a pretty good idea." Joyce replied.

When they reached the street that she lived on, they said their goodbyes. As Joyce walked away, she turned and said "Thank you for the coke, Ed Burk."

Papa just smiled back and waved. He then asked LeeAnn whether she might like to meet her great, great, grandmother and grandfather. "We can easily walk there." He suggested.

"Who are they, as far as relationship?"

"Well, they are my mother's parents. They came to America in 1911 and eventually became citizens here."

"Where did they come from?"

"Poland. That is where my mother's family is from. My father's family came here around the same time from Germany. I lived with my grandparents the first three years of my life. If you can believe it, when I first learned to talk, I only spoke Polish, because that is mostly what my grandparents spoke at home. I also spoke some German."

"Can you still talk Polish or German?"

"No, just a few words and sentences. But it is the strangest thing. I seem to understand what they are saying, even though I no longer speak the language fluently."

"How will I understand them?" LeeAnn asked in a worried tone.

"Oh, not to worry. They speak English, but poorly. People refer to it as 'broken' English. It is common amongst European immigrants. One thing about growing up in Chicago is that the city has areas where people of the same ethnic backgrounds live. So, right now we are entering a Polish neighborhood where the language is spoken freely, even in the stores. It would be the same if we went to Italian or Greek neighborhood. They all talk 'broken' English, but also like to speak their home language."

As they walked, LeeAnn absorbed everything she saw. Despite the city being old, it seemed quite clean. Nowhere was there any graffiti to be seen. Every now and then she would see a garbage can on a corner, and it was obvious it was used as there was no litter anywhere. Being summer, the lack of air conditioning was also obvious, as everyone had their doors open, using only screen doors. She saw people tending their flower gardens and women hanging their clothes on the clothes-lines in the back yards.

It seemed almost every back yard had a dog. Though it was the middle of a summer day, there was no noise to speak of, or music blaring from anywhere.

"For a big city, it's pretty quiet."

"Yeah, it is a different time. People would not think of blasting their music at the neighbors, or blasting it in their cars. You can hear a mother calling for their child from a block away. If a car is loud, the police give them a ticket, so you don't have all the loud vehicles as in 2010."

They approached a neat two-story house, and an old woman was trimming the bushes. When she saw them, she stopped and called "Ed-Veen. What you do here?"

LeeAnn whispered "Why 'Ed-Veen'?"

"Broken English, remember? That's her way of saying Edwin with her accent."

LeeAnn studied her in awe. This was her great, great, grandmother. She was as short as her Nana, barely five feet in height. She embraced Papa and gently cupped his face in her hands, kissing his forehead. For this brief instant, LeeAnn glimpsed her grandfather, as he was as a grandchild. She knew exactly what he was feeling. There Papa stood, wide eyed and filled with happiness, and in this rare moment, they were on equal ground, for she knew the comfort and love he felt. His grandmother smiled broadly. "Ed-Veen you look good. Who is this beautiful girl?"

Papa introduced them. "Grandma, this is my friend LeeAnn."

She looked at LeeAnn up and down. "She is so pretty. She looks like a Polish girl!"

Papa smiled. "Yes Grandma, she is part Polish."

"You are so beautiful." She said to LeeAnn.

"Thank You." LeeAnn was blushing.

"You call me Lottie."

"Where's Jaja?" Papa asked.

"Oh, he keep busy in garage." His grandmother answered in her broken English.

Once again, LeeAnn had a flashback of how she and her sister and cousins always went to Nana first and then always asked "Where's Papa?" *'I guess all grandkids are the same.'*

"You hungry?" She asked.

"No, Grandma, we are fine."

"Is your father taking care of you?" She asked.

"I'm okay, Grandma."

She then turned and mumbled a long phrase in Polish.

"What did she say?" LeeAnn asked.

"You don't want to know. But it had to do with my father."

"I take it she does not like your dad." LeeAnn deducted.

"His own family wants nothing to do with him, so what do you think?"

"I'm sorry Pa…I mean Ed"

"Let's go see your great, great grandfather." As they walked along the side of the house, they were greeted by a large female Doberman Pincher. She stood up and leaned her body on Papa, licking his face. "Oh, you're a good girl. I'm glad to see you too!" He told her. "This is Shauna, by the way. She is a great watchdog and a real sweetie."

Shauna ran ahead, giving her happy bark. Jaja [Grandpa] stuck his head out of the garage door. Quickly he smiled. "Ed-Veen, what you do here? Is Bronia with you?"

Bronia was his name for Bernice, his daughter and Ed's mother. "No Jaja, my friend and I just walked here to say 'hello' and see you for a few minutes. What are you doing?"

"I make bench. You want learn? I teach you."

"Not today Jaja. We have to be going soon as LeeAnn must get home. LeeAnn, this is my Grandpa. I call him Jaja, which is 'Papa' in Polish. His name is Stanley, or in Polish, Stosh."

"Glad to meet you." LeeAnn replied. She studied him, as he was medium in height, but very stocky with huge, strong looking hands. His hair was grey and his smile was warm, but most of all, he had the kindest brown eyes. She immediately liked him.

He smiled and offered "You kids stay. Mama feed you."

"No Jaja, we will soon be on our way."

He reached into his pocket and produced a dollar. "Here Ed-Veen, you take."

"Thanks Jaja." LeeAnn watched as her Papa gave his grandfather a hug. It was more than just a hug, it was an embrace that she knew was deep from Papa's heart. "I'll see you again soon."

LeeAnn watched as her Papa smiled and looked at his grandfather, taking in every second. She realized how precious this visit must actually be to him. Here he was, seeing his grandfather who had passed away over forty years ago. She began to wonder if this was her dream, or was Papa really with her, traveling through time? As they left the garage, one look in his eyes and she knew he was there, as she could see him controlling his tears. She knew they were tears of happiness. Walking back to the front of the house, he bid goodbye to his grandmother in the same manner. His embrace was such that his grandmother asked him.

"Are you sure you okay?"

He held back his tears and assured her. "Yes, Grandma, I'm fine."

They walked away and continued their journey. LeeAnn watched as Papa wiped away his tears.

"I guess you must really be happy to see them?"

He looked at her and smiled. "More than you know."

For almost a block there was silence, and LeeAnn knew Papa was savoring every moment of that visit. She could only imagine what he was feeling. Finally, he spoke.

"So, what do you think?" Papa asked.

"They looked so warm and friendly, but honestly, I did not know what to say. I mean, who gets to meet their great, great grandparents?"

"I guess you're right. They were a wonderful example of what this country once was. They came here when they were young and did not even know English. Jaja, although he made a living doing mostly manual labor, learned quickly and actually speaks three or four languages, so learning English wasn't a problem. They started with nothing, and they raised four children and own their home. All their children finished high school and a few attended trade school or associate college. My uncle Edwin, their son, served in the army in World War II, in which my mom also served."

"Women could join the army way back then?" LeeAnn was shocked.

"Yeah, they called it the WACS. It was the Women's Army Corp, but they could not serve in combat or combat areas. My mom, your great grandmother, served by working in an Army factory, and was awarded a medal for volunteering to ride in experimental airplanes."

"Wow! Have you ever seen the medal?"

"Yes, I have one of them. I also have her uniform."

"One of them? There were more?"

"Yes, she actually was awarded at least three that I know of, plus some ribbons of honor."

"Will I ever see them?"

"I'll make sure you do." Papa stated.

"Papa, tell me about the coins. They're different from what I've ever seen."

"Well, for one thing, the pennies are all copper. Except for the nickels, the rest are silver. Precious metals are just not that valuable in 1956. Gold is only about $35 an ounce, compared with $1400 in 2010. God, I wish I would have saved a few pounds."

"Why did it become so expensive?"

"Now that is complicated subject and someday when you are a bit older, I will explain what happened that changed our whole economy. But hey, right now I'm only ten years old and I don't know squat!"

"Yeah, right!" LeeAnn replied sarcastically.

"I'm not avoiding the subject, but this is 1956 and no one has ever heard of a credit card. It is a cash society with the only common borrowing is for a house or a car."

"No credit?"

"Only some stores have their own 'in-store' type of credit, but there is no universal credit like a Visa or Discover. If you want to borrow, you must go to a bank or loan company."

"Whoa! In 2010, my dad has a bunch of credit cards."

"Well, today he would likely have a wallet filled with money and a bank account with plenty in it! It is a huge difference in times. 1956 was a time when people only purchased what they could well-afford. But let's have some fun! See that store up at the corner? Let me introduce you to penny candy!"

The sign read "B&B Confectionary" and as they approached, LeeAnn could see a steady stream of people leaving and entering the store. Most everyone left holding their purchase in their hand, whether in was cigarettes or a loaf of bread. The old man behind the counter smiled when they entered. "Well, Mister Burk! What can I do for you today?"

"We just want some penny candy." Papa stated.

"What? No empty bottles for me today?" The old man asked.

"Not today. In fact, I have a whole dollar my grandpa gave me."

"Why go for the penny candy? Buy a whole bar for a nickel!"

"Maybe, but I want my friend here to try some of these." He pointed to a glass case with three shelves holding bins of loose candy.

LeeAnn was amazed at the huge selection. Each item had its own little bin. There were malt balls, jaw breakers, pretzels, bubble gum, peppermint sticks and many items she had never seen before, like little wax bottles filled with colored liquids, wax lips, and a wax shaped mustache.

"All this is just a penny?"

"Yes. Some items like the malt balls, you get two for a penny." Papa explained.

LeeAnn looked at the rack of candy bars. "Geez, look at the size of them. What is a Chunky? I never saw a Mars Bar before. What's Beeman's gum?"

"Yeah, we had a lot of things that are long gone in 2010. Some of it was good, but like cigarettes, some of it was not so healthy."

"Mister Ricketts, I'll just take a dimes worth of the top shelf. Pick the first ten items."

"You're the boss young man. Here, I'll throw in a few extra for the young lady."

"Thank you." LeeAnn replied.

"You are so pretty. Is she your cousin?" He asked.

"Yeah, she is visiting from Missouri." Papa quickly replied.

"Well you have a good time here in the city. You stay out of trouble, young man!"

"Yes sir!" Papa responded with a grin that said otherwise. He handed the man his dollar and a got a hand full of change in return.

They left the store and walked along, sampling the candy. LeeAnn seemed to absorb all the sites. She noticed the procession of old panel trucks. "Papa, why are there so many small trucks?"

"You mean the ones that are about the size of small UPS trucks?"

"Yeah."

"Well, that's because almost everything can be home-delivered. You will see these trucks for delivery of milk, cleaning and laundry, diaper service and more."

LeeAnn stopped him. "Diaper service?"

Papa laughed. "Yeah, disposable diapers have not been invented yet."

"You've got to be kidding!"

"No, I'm not!"

LeeAnn made a face. "How does that work?"

"Well, each house that has the service gets a hamper, and when the baby uses the diaper, they put it in the hamper. The service picks up the dirty diapers and delivers a clean supply."

LeeAnn laughed. "Man, I bet that truck smells!"

"That driver probably gets paid pretty good. He better." As they walked, a paper truck pulled up and the driver threw a bundle of papers on the sidewalk.

"Why did he just dump them?"

"Likely it is for that store, and the owner will come out and get them."

"No one will steal them?"

"Nah. Who wants a pile of papers?"

"Everything seems so active..." LeeAnn observed.

"Like how?"

"Well, other than our main shopping mall, when we go to a small strip mall, you never see this kind of activity. Everywhere I look there are people going in and out. There always seems to be people walking or crossing the streets everywhere."

"It's the times. We had no one stop shopping. People used to make lists of places they had to visit or shop at. Maybe the butcher shop, then the bakery, then the drug store, etc. Maybe add the tailor, the cleaners, the shoe repair and more. In fact, Saturday's are almost exclusively reserved for running errands all day. One thing about this time period, is things got fixed. Shoes got repaired. Clothes got resized or repaired, as fashions were not as fleeting. You see that kid over there with those patches on his jeans? That is not a fashion statement; it is because he wore the knees out and the patches cover the holes. Almost all appliances, including the small ones like toasters, were repaired. It was not a 'throw away' generation, and obsolescence was not much of a factor. In 2010, people always seem to be tossing things out and waiting for the next best thing."

"People do seem happier. I see lots of smiles." LeeAnn replied.

"Sure, there are no cell phones or beepers or texting or credit cards, and there is a lot less stress. Choices are simple, as there are few. Everything makes sense. You know why they call business people 'white collar workers?' Simply because if you work in any office, whether bank or private business, men only wear white shirts and ties. Life is simple. If we go into the men's store and I ask for a dress shirt, they only have white. If I go to the shoe store, I have a choice of laces or loafers in black or brown--sometimes oxblood--and that's about it."

"What's oxblood?"

"It's like a reddish brown"

"I am confused, because in some ways, I like having more choices, yet I can see how less stressful it is having less to deal with."

"Well I can tell you with confidence that no one is waiting for anything to be released next month that will change their world. The only thing people await is the fall when they release the new model cars. Aside from that, life goes on. People have more time to talk, or visit the library, or attend church. There is a lot less peer-pressure. Look at the next ten boys we cross paths with. Most likely they are all wearing jeans and a tee shirt, and are wearing either black gym shoes or loafers. No one cares what the labels are."

"Yeah, I guess that would kind of change things."

"Do me a favor. Watch your parents when you go home. See how it compares to what they normally go through in 2010."

"Papa, what will we do tomorrow?"

"Have you ever climbed a fire escape?"

"What's that?"

Papa laughed. "You'll see. Have you ever ridden on top of a real train?"

"No way!"

"We'll see!"

As they approached LeeAnn's apartment, they paused for a moment and LeeAnn looked at Papa seriously. "Do you promise I can still be here tomorrow?"

For a brief second, she could see the wisdom in his eyes. "Yes, I promise. Now get on home and remember to watch your parents. I want a report!"

Around the corner he went, smiling as he ran. LeeAnn had her assignment and she would take it seriously. '*What is a fire escape?'* She wondered.

Chapter Five

LeeAnn opened the front door and it was unlocked as usual. She just found that to be so very strange! As she entered, she immediately noticed her dad, sitting in what was likely his favorite chair, reading a book. She paused and observed that he seemed so relaxed and at peace. She turned into the kitchen and her mom was busy cooking and playing the radio, while singing along to a song she did not recognize; but was, in her mind, surely an 'oldie'.

She did exactly what Papa asked of her, and observed how happy they both appeared. She hardly ever saw her dad reading a book, for in 2010, he was always busy; either on the computer, in the garage, or in the yard. What she saw with her mom was also amazing, as her mom was smiling and seemed to enjoy creatively preparing that evening's dinner. Her mom did not seem stressed, or in any kind of hurry. She noticed the phone was silent and the television was turned off. She glanced at the dining room table and observed another strange sight; it was a puzzle. A huge number of pieces were spread about, and only a portion of the border was assembled.

"What's this mom?"

"Oh, your dad bought us a new puzzle. Go on--try to put a few pieces together. This is a tough one." Her mom replied.

"Wow, how many pieces is this thing?"

"I think it's about two thousand pieces."

LeeAnn was perplexed. "Are we going to have to put it together tonight?"

"No, dear. As always, we'll just leave it there and each of us will put parts together whenever we have a little time."

LeeAnn took a seat and began trying to match up a few pieces after looking at the picture on the box. What she did not know, was that this was a most common past time in the fifties.

"What's for dinner?"

"Meatloaf, mashed potatoes and green beans."

"Yum!"

"Honey, will you bring me a beer?" Her dad yelled.

She watched as her mom brought a bottle to her dad, who replied "Thanks, dear." as he continued reading. LeeAnn noticed the label on the bottle which read 'Blatz.'

'Blatz? Dad only drinks Bud? What's with that?' LeeAnn wondered, not knowing Blatz beer was very popular in Chicago in the fifties. As she focused on the puzzle, it seemed so unusual that there was such silence; an abnormal calm the likes of which she had never known. Suddenly, she found a piece that fit in the border. "I found one!" she yelled.

"Great, sweetie!" her dad responded.

Having a slight feeling of accomplishment, she focused on searching out another piece. As she did, she also became aware that this puzzle, which was something she had never done, was actually fun. *'Do they still have these?'* She wondered.

Time just seemed to stand still as she concentrated, but soon her mom broke the silence calling "Dinner time!"

As she went to the kitchen, her mom reminded her. "Wash your hands, young lady."

As she washed, she became aware that she had not heard a swear word in days; which, unfortunately, was all too common in 2010, even on television. She proceeded to the kitchen table, where her dad was smiling. "This looks great and smells even better!"

"Thank you, sweetheart."

LeeAnn was a bit in awe, for she had no memory of her parents interacting in such a caring fashion. She knew that, obviously, they were once in love, but her memories were only those of negative emotion.

"Wall Street thinks the DOW average will hit 500 again this month. The economy is really starting to soar. My company is thinking of opening a new facility in St. Louis." Her dad stated.

"Missouri is a great state!" LeeAnn responded without thinking.

"How would you know that?" He asked.

Pausing for an answer, LeeAnn replied. "We studied it in school." Then she made a huge blunder. "Yeah, they have a giant arch."

"A what?" Her dad asked.

"An arch?" LeeAnn stated timidly.

"What is an arch? Where is an arch?" He asked.

LeeAnn immediately knew she goofed, as likely the St. Louis Arch had not yet been built.

"I don't really know. It's just something I heard."

"Well, maybe it is some kind of landmark or something. I'll grab the encyclopedia and look it up later and see if it even exists."

It was at that moment that LeeAnn realized how many books were scattered about. On top of the newspaper crossword puzzle on the kitchen counter, was a dictionary. Over on a chair was a Reader's Digest. From her seat she could see a bookcase filled with books, which was likely an entire set of encyclopedias. Next to her dad's chair was an end table with a book and magazine rack built-in, and it was filled. She could understand what an important part books played before computers existed.

Dinner was delicious. It was much better than anything her mom had ever made. "This is great, Mom!"

"Thank you. It is another new recipe from Home and Garden magazine."

"This is one to keep!" Her dad replied. He then added. "The Cubs are having a terrible year. It looks like no playoffs this time. Brooklyn Dodgers appear unbeatable."

'*Brooklyn?*' LeeAnn wondered, as she never heard the name before in regards to baseball.

As they ate dinner, a sudden sadness came over LeeAnn, as she realized that this scenario could never really exist in her world. Her parents have been divorced for a few years and both were contemplating getting remarried to other people in the near future. For a moment, she wished that this situation could be real. If only her sister Ashlee could be here to see this.

"Are you going out after dinner?" Her mom asked.

"Nah, I think I'll work on that puzzle and go to bed early."

LeeAnn was anxious to greet a new day and see what adventures Papa had in store for her. As was her habit, she started collecting the dishes as her dad lit a cigar. '*Blatz beer? Smoking cigars? Weird.*'

As she worked on the puzzle, she was aware of how her parents were so laid back and relaxed. They were both laughing as they watched someone called 'Jack Benny'. Her mom had a pretty wooden box that contained yarn, and was knitting as she watched television. LeeAnn wondered '*Did my parents ever get along this well?*' She knew she would never forget this moment, even if it was a dream. She sat, finding pieces to the puzzle, until she found herself yawning. Then she walked to front room to say goodnight. Instead of usual quick 'G-night,' she hugged her dad tightly and whispered "I love you, Dad." She then went to her mom and did the same, saying "I love you, Mom."

Walking to her room, she could hear her mom whisper "Is she okay?"

"Yeah, I'm sure she is fine. She just looked a little tired." Dad assumed.

After washing up and brushing her teeth, she was soon snuggled in and fast asleep. Her last thoughts were wondering what the next day might bring. She slept soundly and learned that one cannot have dreams if they are already in dreams. So it seemed as though she had just shut her eyes when her mom called to her.

"Are you going to sleep all day?"

"What time is it, Mom?"

"Well, it's almost nine and I'm leaving for work, so there's some cereal on the table. Bye, honey!"

After washing up and getting dressed, she sat at the kitchen table eating her cereal when she heard a soft knock on the open screen door. It was Papa. "You ready?"

"Yeah! What are we doing today?"

"Well, you said the nice lady next door would allow us to take some bottles, so that's first. We can add that to our cash." She could see Papa eyeing the empty bottles. "**When I was your age,** this was considered a treasure!"

"Cool!" LeeAnn replied. She put her bowl in the sink, and soon they were picking out bottles.

"Just take the quart pop bottles, or else we have to go into a tavern with the beer bottles. This way, we can take them to the grocery store." He explained.

They took as many as they could carry and went to the corner grocery store. A minute later, they each had a shinny quarter in their hands.

"What's next?" LeeAnn asked.

"I think I will show you how to climb a fire escape and share with you one of my secret places."

They began walking along Armitage Avenue, and LeeAnn almost felt she belonged. With all the little stores and people scurrying about, it resembled Main Street at Disneyworld. Strange people smiled and waved, and she found herself smiling and waving back with no concern. "Papa, were you ever afraid walking this city alone?"

"Not much at this age. More when I was a teenager. Then it became a gang or neighborhood thing. Teens became very territorial. Actually, that is how all the city gangs got started. They were organized to protect their neighborhoods. Originally, gangs were ethnically defined, as Chicago is an ethnic melting pot. All these neighborhoods are predominately one nationality. Where we are now, is mostly German and Polish working class. As a child, I only had one time that I can remember that frightened me."

"What was it?" LeeAnn asked anxiously, thinking it would be dangerous or maybe even ghostly.

"Well, it was about ten o'clock at night last year around Halloween, and I was out late and sitting on the steps of a store. I saw a big man walking down the street and when he got close, he was wearing clown make-up! For some reason, it scared me. It was just so creepy. Honestly, I don't know if it was a costume or disguise, but it freaked me out. Even as I grew older, people in make-up freak me out. I just really hate clowns."

LeeAnn began laughing. "So a big clown scared you?" She giggled.

"Well a grown man walking around in clown make-up is just plain creepy."

LeeAnn began laughing.

"Hey, it was a bit frightening."

LeeAnn kept laughing. "Papa is afraid of clowns!" Just the thought, to LeeAnn, was hysterical.

"What? You don't think a guy in make-up is scary?"

LeeAnn kept laughing. "Clowns and midgets, that's funny!"

"Okay, I'm also afraid of midgets too! Why is that so funny? They creep me out." He stated with conviction.

"I can't believe it? Papa, you walk the city alone at night and you fear clowns and midgets? You slay me! What about Nana? She is almost a midget? Are you scared of her?"

"Nah, your Nana is not a midget. She is over the limit. She is five feet tall." He replied.

"What about little Oscar?" LeeAnn laughed.

"As long as he stays in the wiener mobile, I'm okay with him! But I won't go near him."

"In fact, anyone in disguise disturbs me. I feel they are hiding something. Even the entertainers that try to look like other entertainers make me uncomfortable. It is like they are hiding who they truly are, and some seem like they have lost their true identity. We have a guy in Branson that does an Elvis show. The problem is, he never leaves his Elvis persona behind, and even has had plastic surgery to look more like Elvis. Even in the 'off' season, he walks around town acting like Elvis. I always wonder when he looks in the mirror, who does he really see? These people are just not right. And clowns? When you are a little older, I'll tell about John Wayne Gacey. He was quite a clown."

"Tell me, Papa!"

"No, not until you're a little older."

"Papa, what could be so bad?"

"He was a serial killer, and that's all I'll say."

"Oh." LeeAnn gasped.

Soon, LeeAnn found they were walking away from the street and between buildings. They were soon behind a large brick building when Papa pointed upward.

"See that?"

LeeAnn gazed up at an iron stairway built onto the outside of the building.

"That's a fire escape."

"I've seen these before in the movies."

He explained further. "They are only used for emergencies, but they are great for getting up on roofs." He stepped back, and with a running start, he jumped high enough to grab onto a set of stairs. They had a counter weight that kept them suspended off the ground. As Papa hung on, the stairway slowly lowered. "Come on!" He motioned. They began walking up six stories. When they reached the top floor, there was a ladder going to the roof. LeeAnn hesitated.

"Papa, this is dangerous."

"Yes, it could be, but not in my dreams. If you want, you can even jump from here. You can never be harmed. Trust me. Besides, we have a staircase and a ladder; do you think this is anywhere near as dangerous as modern day rock climbing?"

They climbed to the roof, and as they reached the top, they surprised a flock of pigeons that immediately took to the sky. "This is actually a grain factory, but I call it the pigeon factory. You can see why."

There were huge stainless steel vents that made for a perfect bench. From there, they could see over the roof tops for miles. LeeAnn was used to heights from growing up in the Ozark Mountains, so she enjoyed the view without fear.

"Sometimes, I would come here alone. I'd often bring food or a drink and watch the sunset. It's not as beautiful as the Ozarks, but it was beautiful to me at the time. See that factory over there? That's the Pepsi factory. Sometimes I go over there and get a free Pepsi."

"How do you do that?"

"See all those cases of bottles behind the factory? Most times, there is at least one case with full bottles. I simply climb the fence and search one out. Although, it's best to go inside, because their machine is only a nickel, and the Pepsi is so cold that the bottles have ice chips on the inside."

"They let you do that?"

"Sure. The employees are all very nice to kids."

"See over there? Those are the railroad tracks, where slow freight trains pass by. Some have over a hundred cars. Whether coming or going, they are always moving slowly. Going towards the city, they are slowing down before they reach the railroad yard and leaving, it takes them twenty miles to build up speed."

"Boy, those must stop traffic!"

"Well, Chicago is pretty smart, and most streets dip under the railroad tracks. We call them viaducts. So traffic is not generally affected. Chicago is the railroad center of the country. Get ready, because we will ride one today."

"Really?"

"Sure. When a long one comes by, all you need to do is jump on in the middle of the train. This way the engineer in the front, and the guy in the caboose can't see you."

"Caboose?" LeeAnn began laughing. "Caboose, that sounds funny."

"The caboose is the last car on the train. It is most always painted red. Yeah, I have used the word in a funny way, like I will kick someone in their caboose!"

LeeAnn laughed loudly. "Papa, you're hysterical."

"Seriously, I don't really know exactly what the purpose is, but I know there are men riding inside the caboose that are like watchmen. I had one yell at me once."

"Has anyone ever chased you off this roof?"

"Never. I really never have seen anyone here. I always had the feeling that they worked at night."

"Papa, if they only work at night, maybe they are vampires!" LeeAnn joked.

"Ah, I'll kick them in the caboose!"

LeeAnn laughed at the very thought. "Papa, you're too small to kick anyone in the caboose! Did you know you would grow up to be so big?"

"Nah, I had no clue."

"Well, I saw your grandmother and grandfather, and I have seen pictures of your mom and dad, and no one is anywhere near as big as you."

"Honestly, it was always a mystery to me, until I saw a picture of my grandmother's parents."

"Was your great grandfather a big man?"

"No, he was almost a darned midget, but my great grandmother on my mother's side was huge! I have an old picture and she is sitting down with her husband, my great grandfather, standing next to her. Even sitting down, she is taller! She was well over six feet! I will have to show you the old photo."

"It is just the opposite of you and Nana!"

"Yeah. I felt sorry for him. I'll bet she really kicked his caboose."

LeeAnn laughed uncontrollably, not knowing how her Papa was basking in the glow of her happiness. He observed her as she took in the sites of the city, when suddenly her smile faded.

"What?" He asked.

"Papa, when I see my mom and dad together, I can't help but get sad. I will never see them like this again. They seem so happy."

"Sweetie, they once were very, very happy, believe me. Somehow, they parted ways. As you get older, you will find more than half the children you will meet will also come from broken homes. Divorce has become all too common in 2010. Most parents are not as caring as yours. Your parents at least work together as best they can and are always concerned with your best interests. **When I was your age,** divorce was unheard of and frowned on. So I was kind of unique. All my friends had their parents together. In a way, I was labeled as a bad influence, because--as you can see--I was able to do what I wanted…for a while, anyway."

"Why only for a while? What changed?"

"Later this year, my father will leave me on my own, and I will get the flu and pneumonia, and will nearly die. You see, we have no antibiotics, other than penicillin. Afterward, when I recover, the state will take me and put me in a Catholic children's institution. There, I will stay until I graduate eighth grade."

"That had to be horrible." LeeAnn gasped. "You nearly died from just the flu?"

"Sure. Thousands of children died from the flu before modern drugs were discovered and developed. I lost one of my little brothers to a form of meningitis."

"Your little brother died?"

"Yeah. That is why I can't take you to see my mom, because you will meet my little brother, Butch, and it will only bring you sadness."

"When did he die?"

"Later this year, 1956."

"How old was he?"

"About 3 and a half."

"I'm so sorry, Papa. Did he suffer at all?"

"Actually, I would like to think not, as he went very fast. He became sick and it looked like some kind of stomach problem. The doctor had my mom take him to the hospital, and that was the last time I saw him."

"So your brother died, and then they put you in an institution? How did you handle being taken away?"

"It felt horrible at the time, but as I grew older, I realized it was the best thing that could have happened. You will find that certain things in your life will be the same. It may appear that they are negatives at the time, but some of those will build your character and make you stronger."

"So being in an institution is not a bad memory?"

"Just the opposite. I was educated, safe, well fed, and learned so many things. Had I stayed on the streets like I am today, I likely would eventually have gotten into ten kinds of trouble. Don't judge your future by what you are feeling today."

"Papa, how did you know that Nana was special, and how did you stay together all these years?"

"Maybe ask me this question a few years from now, as you might better understand. For now, I can only say we needed each other. Now that sounds simple, but it's not. I can add that we had nothing to get in our way. We didn't have much; only hopes for building a future. Neither of us had great childhoods, and neither of us even had a place that we could call home, so we both knew that life was tough, and we would face it together. Everything we accomplished made our lives better. Our expectations were wide open, so money, cars, houses, and all the material things never became obstacles. One thing I promise you; never will your true happiness be based on material things, and never judge a person by what they have."

"Papa, I can see a train coming."

"Yeah, it's about ten minutes away. We've got plenty of time. Let's head down."

As they climbed the ladder down to the fire escape stairway, Papa told LeeAnn. "On the last set of stairs, just walk out there real quick, and you will ride down like a teeter-tauter. It's a great feeling. It's like you're floating on air."

Slowly and cautiously she walked out onto the suspended stairs, and just as Papa said, they began lowering, giving her a floating feeling. "This is great!"

When they reached the ground, they walked toward the railroad tracks. There was no fence or barriers, and no warning signs. LeeAnn was slightly surprised by this. "Papa, can anyone just walk up here?"

"Really, it's no big deal; we are merely standing near a moving train. Is this any different than standing on a street corner with cars speeding by at 40 MPH?"

"So we are really going to jump on?"

"Yes. All we will do is wait until about twenty-five cars pass and then we will run alongside and grab onto the ladder on the side of the freight car. We will climb the ladder and sit on the roof."

"How will we get off?" LeeAnn was concerned.

"About a mile or so down is a soft grassy area. We will climb down the ladder and jump."

"Won't we get hurt?"

"Not in my dreams. Besides, if you know how to tumble, it's no big deal."

"Tumble?"

"Have you not had tumbling in gym class?"

"Uh, no. What is that?"

"It is the art of learning to fall, or to jump. You are taught how to roll, and how to bend your legs. You are taught how to do summersaults and that stuff. It is like a form of gymnastics." He explained.

"Well I know how to do a summersault, but we never had anything called tumbling."

"Well, looks like you might just land on your caboose!"

"Come on Papa! I'm scared."

"Not to worry. The train will be going so slow, you won't have a problem. I promise."

"I'm worried about jumping off."

"It's nothing, as it will only be going a few miles an hour. You know what you should do? You should ask your dad to show you some of the video clips that people post on the web. Have him show you the skate board accidents. You will see these idiots trying to jump hand rails and crashing at 30 MPH. They get concussions, break their legs, and meet the concrete face first; some even wind up paralyzed. Believe me, this is a lot safer than skateboarding." Papa laughed. "You know, almost everything we are surrounded with today is gone and determined too dangerous, yet I watched a video of a kid who rode his snowboard right off a cliff! I also saw one of a kid that tried to ride his bike off the roof of his house! Idiots are idiots! You can't keep idiots from harming themselves. **When I was your age,** we may have been surrounded with dangers, but we had the common sense to avoid them. We certainly didn't seek them out."

They sat behind some bushes as the train slowly passed. LeeAnn could see the engineer looking out from the huge locomotive pulling the train. Papa sat, watching and counting the freight cars. When he counted twenty-five, he announced "Just run along with me and grab onto one of the ladders on the side."

LeeAnn was surprised to find the train was going slow enough that she could easily run with it. She watched Papa grab onto the ladder, and she did the exact same thing. She jumped up and was soon riding the ladder. Papa yelled to her. "Climb to the top!" She did, and now they were riding the roof of the box car.

She was so excited that she began laughing. "Papa, this is great!"

"Sit down and enjoy the ride." He replied.

LeeAnn had never ridden on a real train, much less the roof of a freight car, so she felt as though she had accomplished something exciting and dangerous.

"Papa, you did this all the time?"

"Yeah, I have ridden one of these completely out of the city. I was never afraid, because Grand Avenue runs parallel to these tracks and my father used to drive this route since I was real small, so even if I couldn't catch a train back, I could hop on the back of a truck and return that way. None of this is anything one could even try in 2010."

LeeAnn just sat and stared out at the buildings moving passed. She noticed that a few people saw them and even waved. "Papa, this is fun!"

"We are going to jump off soon, because I don't want to take you too far."

"Come on Papa, can't we ride a little longer?"

"You like this, do you? Too bad we don't have snow, I could take you skitching."

"What's skitching?"

"Skitching is a word that combines skiing with hitching, as in hitching a ride. In the winter, the streets become covered with ice. Cars, for the most part, drive very slow. When they stop for a red light, you sneak behind and grab onto the back bumper and just hang on. It's like sledding, without the sled. It is really a lot of fun."

"What about the cars behind you? If you let go, won't they run you over?"

"Well, for one thing, you don't do it in rush hour, for Pete's sake! You wait until a lone car--or better yet, a bus--comes by. You always stay to the curb side of the car and slide off in that direction if you have to. Maybe it's a little dangerous, but it's a lot of fun!"

"Did your parents ever know what you were doing?"

"Not a chance. My dad probably wouldn't care, but my mom would have gone crazy and punished the heck out of me. Come on, climb down the ladder and watch me, then do the same. When you land, let your legs bend so you can fall and roll."

LeeAnn climbed down the ladder and the sound of the steel wheels rolling on the tracks was deafening. She watched Papa and jumped immediately after he did. She rolled onto the grass and could not hold back her exhilaration. "Wow! That was too cool! Almost like something from the movies!"

"We only rode a mile or so, do you want to wait and ride back or walk?"

"Can we walk? This way we can talk some." LeeAnn suggested.

Suddenly, they heard a sound like Christmas bells, and the musical sound of a dozen little chiming bells filled the air.

"What is that?" LeeAnn asked.

"That's the Good Humor Man!"

"Good Humor? What is that?"

"Just the best ice cream around!" Papa answered, grinning.

"You can buy it on the street?"

"Yes, he drives through the neighborhoods. Look; here comes the truck!"

LeeAnn watched as the gleaming white truck stopped and kids came running to buy their ice cream from a man who was also in all white. Just a minute later, she and Papa were enjoying ice cream bars as they continued their walk.

"Okay, what's on your mind?"

"Did your mom get married again?"

"No, she never did."

"Did she ever tell you why?"

"Yeah. As a 'divorcee,' she felt that she never wanted to take a chance that the man she married might not treat us children well. My father may have ruined her, as far as men were concerned. Besides, she was a very independent woman and was a little before her time."

"How so?"

"Well, at a time when women did not work, she loved working. She also liked handling her own financial affairs, even though we were poor. She taught me that you must always live within your means and only buy what you can pay for. Her favorite saying was 'Never drink Champagne from a paper cup."

"I don't understand?"

"It's like saying 'Don't buy a car if you can't afford the gas'. Or better yet, 'Don't buy an iPod, if you can't afford the downloads."

"Oh, I get it."

"Yeah, she pounded that into my head and although she did not have a great education, she left me with some great lessons and basic life philosophies that have served me well. That and my religious education really helped me throughout my life."

"I don't have a lot of religious education." LeeAnn admitted.

Papa just smiled. "You will."

"How do you know?"

"When you are a bit older, you will seek it out yourself."

"How do you know that, Papa?"

"Because I do. You will soon recognize that there is a higher power guiding you. All you must do is listen."

"It sounds like you are talking about something supernatural?"

"It certainly is. You likely already have a guardian angel and don't even know it."

"You're kidding. Right?"

"Let me ask you this. Have you ever had a little voice or feeling pushing you in a direction? Sort of pointing you toward something?"

"Like how?"

"Oh, like telling you not to walk to school a certain way, or maybe not to do something? Not really a voice but a strong feeling that almost controls you. Maybe a feeling that says 'stay away from that person,' for no reason you can understand?"

"You mean like a feeling that says don't go out in the yard when it is dark sometimes? Or don't open the door for a strange person?"

"Exactly."

"Yeah, I have had those feelings."

"As you get older, if you listen, you will sense them more often and they will become stronger. They might tell you to go to a certain school for college, or to not go to that party. They might even say to take a certain job. They can guide you to avoid bad things and to move toward good things. I have so many instances of that in my life, and as you get older, I will share many with you; but God can play a big part in your life--if you allow him."

"But Papa, I never knew you went to church."

"I really haven't for years, but you need not go to church to talk with God."

"Really?"

"Please, don't think I'm saying not to go to church; but God is all around you. If I pray right here, right now, is it any less meaningful?"

"Uh, I don't think so."

"That is my only point. I pray every morning and every night, sincerely and from my heart. Many times I pray in my own words, rather than traditional prayers. Most people think God only listens to prayers from a church or from a hospital bed. Somehow, I think it is more important when you pray in private on your own personal time and not because you're in trouble, or that you must because it's been scheduled. I learned to pay attention and trust those inner feelings. It was that little voice when I was a musician that told me not to travel on a job to New York, even though it paid more, and instead, take a path that led me to Tulsa, where I met your Nana. Because of that, you are here! Is that not a miracle?"

LeeAnn giggled, "Well I can't deny that, can I? Papa, how can we be doing this right here, right now?"

"That I cannot explain until the time is right. For now, I can only tell you it is a gift."

"What are we going to do next?"

"What would you like to do?"

"I know you didn't want me to, but could I meet my great grandmother, your mom?"

"Funny you asked, because that is the direction we are going. You know you will meet your Uncle Butch, who will die soon."

"I met my great, great, grandparents and handled it okay, didn't I?"

"So be it."

Soon they approached a large apartment building. "We will have to go up to the third floor." When they reached the top of the stairs, Papa opened the door and yelled "Mom?" She came out from the kitchen, carrying an infant.

She instantly smiled. "Ed!" She hugged him as best she could while holding the baby. "Are you okay?"

"Yeah mom, I'm fine."

"Where are you and your father living?"

"We are over on Kimbal and Armitage."

"You want something to eat?"

"Nah, I'm full mom."

"Who is your friend?"

"This is LeeAnn. We go to school together."

Running out from a bedroom came the little brother, Butch. "Ed!" He screamed. He was smiling, and ran up to Papa, expecting his big brother to catch him.

"Man Butchie, you weight a ton!" LeeAnn watched as Papa grabbed Butchie's baby fat. "You're a chubby chub!" Butch laughed. It was a loud, infectious laugh that made LeeAnn smile.

"Who is she, Ed?" Butch asked.

"This is LeeAnn. My friend."

"Hi…" Butch said shyly.

Watching television and paying absolutely no attention, was Papa's sister, Candace. "Hello Candy!" he yelled.

"Hi, Ed…" she yelled back, without even turning her head.

"Are you coming home?" Butch asked.

"No, little guy, I must stay with dad for a while."

A sad look came over him. "I want you home!"

LeeAnn watched as Papa ran his hand along the side of Butchie's face, as if rekindling a memory. "I'll be home soon, I promise."

Butch smiled. "Hug!" he demanded.

LeeAnn could hardly watch as Papa hugged little Butch and held back his tears. "I love you, little man." Papa whispered.

"I love you too, Ed." Butch smiled.

Papa pointed to the baby. "This is my brother, Joe."

LeeAnn tickled his cheek and he smiled. “He is so cute!”

“Mom, is everything okay?” Ed asked.

“Well, you know your father.” She replied in a disgusted tone. “If he comes home tonight, ask him to remember the child support. He is three weeks behind.”

“Like he will listen to me?” Papa responded. “I’ll do it if he isn’t drunk.”

Papa kissed his mom on the cheek. “Mom, we’re on our way to the park, but I wanted LeeAnn to meet you and my brothers and sister.”

“You take care, Ed.”

“I will mom…I will.”

LeeAnn watched as Papa turned back one last time and gave what was a sad farewell. “Bye Mom. Bye Butch.”

They turned and left, bounding down the stairs. LeeAnn could not help but say “Your mom treated you almost like an adult.”

“Yeah, it was always that way. As I got older, I was responsible for the family and it just came natural. I may be only ten, but mom and I have gone through a lot together.”

As they walked, LeeAnn remained silent. This experience actually made her feel a little bit lucky that her mom and dad, although divorced, were good and caring parents. Papa was also silent and she was not sure whether he was filled with happiness at seeing his family again, or sadness of reliving the circumstances.

“Come on, let’s go get a hot dog and eat in the park.” Papa suggested.

They walked to a hot dog stand that was not much more than an old trailer parked in an empty lot.

“Two dogs and fries and two cokes, please.”

“That’s 71 cents.” The man yelled as he made up the hot dogs and dropped the fries into the hot oil.

Papa produced a dollar from his pocket. “You’ll love these. I could eat a bag of these fries alone.”

The man produced two brown bags containing the hot dogs and what appeared to LeeAnn as two pounds of French fries, plus two small bottles of coke. Papa pocketed his change and suggested “Let’s head over to the park.”

As they walked, LeeAnn reminded Papa “You know, I prefer root beer.”

“Yes, and I prefer Pepsi, but that guy only sells Cokes. Most of these little places serve Pepsi or Coke, and rarely do they offer flavors. Diet drinks do not even exist, and neither does bottled water. In fact, if anyone suggested bottling water today, they would be laughed at. You can see that there is no such thing as plastic bottles. Everything is glass."

When they reached the park, they sat on a bench in the shade. After the day they had experienced, LeeAnn was starving. For a while, they sat quietly, eating. LeeAnn assumed after what he had relived, that Papa was in deep thought. Eventually he looked toward her and asked "So? What did you think?"

"Lots of things. For one, your poor mom…how does she live without your dad helping?"

"My mom is a genius at stretching a dollar, and if I know her, she has a small amount saved. It's not like my dad's lack of responsibility is not common knowledge. The one thing you can count on, is that you can never count on him."

"How did you cope?"

"This is what this whole journey is about. At ten years old, you are left with a lot of insecurities. I know what you are feeling, and you can now see that things could be much worse. **When I was your age,** I felt the same way you are feeling. Although you are still considered a child, you are beginning to see things as an adult. You realize you have no control over your immediate destiny. It's a horrible feeling of helplessness. The only future you see is the present day, and the fact that you really don't know what tomorrow brings. You see your parents bringing, what are to you, strangers into your life. You can see how life was for me and now you can compare that to how my life actually turned out. Yes, I experienced a lot of sadness and insecurities, but that never defined the direction my life would take once I became an adult. There will come a time all too soon, when you will take complete control."

"I think I understand." LeeAnn said seriously.

"The most important thing is to become as educated and as strong as you can be. Your parents are just human. Sometimes they will teach you what to do, like my mom teaching me to live within my means. Sometimes your parents, through their behavior, will teach you what not to do, as in my father's drinking. Just know that your time will come, and you should continue to build yourself up to where you are prepared to take charge of your life."

"Well, I do get depressed sometimes, because I wish things were different. I wish my parents were together. Sometimes I cry." LeeAnn admitted.

"I used to cry myself to sleep an awful lot. It's nothing to be ashamed of. By the time I was 12, I think I ran out of tears. Just realize that nothing you see or experience will dictate how you will run your own life. Only you know what you are cataloging in your memory. With me, since my father was violent and beat his children, I understood the pain and would never do that to my children. Because my mom and dad separated and I bounced back and forth, I made sure that the woman I married was someone I would definitely spend my life with, and kept from moving and having my children change schools. I learned what to do, and maybe more importantly, a lot of what not to do."

"Didn't these things affect you at all?"

"Sure. In some ways, your Papa is completely crazy."

LeeAnn laughed. "Like, how?"

"Well, since I never had my own bedroom, I must have a huge bedroom. Since I never had my own closet, I like lots of closets. Since I was always standing in line for the bathroom, Nana and I have four bathrooms for two people. Now you must admit that's a little crazy. Your Nana could give you a list as long as your arm about how eccentric I am. Plus, I am obsessive compulsive. I hide my OC well, but it is something I cope with."

"Do you wash your hands or skip over the cracks in sidewalks?" She chuckled.

"No, I have my own unique compulsions. For one, with certain items I feel I can't do without, I must have at least two of them. Look around our house, you will see it. I have two cameras exactly alike. Two beard trimmers. Our house is filled with multiples. Because I went years with torn, flimsy, worn out winter coat, my closet has at least six or more. There is no exact formula; I just go with what compels me."

"You only have one piano." She quickly stated.

"Wrong, little one. I have a full size keyboard hidden in my closet." Papa replied.

"Really?"

"You can bet on it."

LeeAnn laughed, "What about having two Nana's?"

"No, there is only one and not another like her." He smiled.

"Papa, were you always joking about stuff?"

"Unfortunately, yes. I always tried to laugh regardless of the situation

I was in. I say unfortunately, because all too often it got me in trouble. Come on, let's get you home."

"Papa, what will we do tomorrow?"

"We will talk. In fact, we will talk a lot."

He walked LeeAnn to her apartment and she watched as Papa walked away. He was walking slower this time, but holding his head high. She wondered what this whole experience was like for him. Though it was an adventure for her, she felt it must be a bit painful for her grandfather. She always knew him as being fun and filled with laughter, never knowing the sadness he held inside. What became so very obvious was that this ten year old street kid, who cashed in bottles and stole change from paper stands to survive, could go on to be an executive and retire years early, surrounded by a loving family. She was now armed with a whole new optimism.

This time she opened the front door and thought nothing of it being unlocked. "Hi, Mom!" she yelled.

"Hurry, you will miss Mickey Mouse Club!" Her mom responded.

LeeAnn turned on the TV in time to hear the now familiar theme song. 'M-I-C-K-E-Y...M-O-U-S-E.' Although so very dated, she enjoyed watching the black and white program. Once again, her mom brought her some milk and cookies as a snack. LeeAnn watched her mom went about preparing dinner and seemed so very happy. She was anxious for her dad to arrive. When the program was over, she went to the dining room table to see if she could fit a few more pieces into the giant puzzle. As she concentrated on finding a piece, her eyes grew very heavy, and just for a moment, she felt she could rest her head. Soon, she was fast asleep.

Chapter Six

LeeAnn had begun to awake but was so comfortable snuggled under the soft down quilt. It took a few seconds for her to realize *'How did I get into bed, when I was working on the puzzle?'* A peek from out under the covers told her exactly what had occurred. Her first glimpse was of the nightstand and her iPod. She immediately sat up, and knew her dream was over. She thought about Papa's last words when she asked what they would do the next day. His response was *'Talk; we'll talk a lot.'* She knew it was his way of avoiding telling her that the journey was over. *'But it was so real!'* She had missed her sister Ashlee, but was sad at the exciting world she left behind. She had hopes of seeing Joyce again and of riding the train once more. *'I wonder if we ever finished that puzzle?'* Normally, the first thing she did was reach for her iPod, but today it did not seem all that important. By the faint light coming through the window, she knew it was very early, but she could hear things moving about downstairs. *'Nana is up!'* She quickly ran to bathroom and prepared to shower before getting dressed. *'Can't wait to talk to Papa.'*

As she showered, she realized how many everyday things that always went unnoticed and taken for granted. She was standing in a whirlpool tub, taking a shower that rained down from an oversized showerhead. She was surrounded by shampoos, liquid shower gel, conditioner and other soaps. Over the vanity cabinet were a string of makeup lights. On the vanity was body spray, perfumed talcum powder, hair spray. All this was very different from where she had just visited.

When finished, she walked around, observing the second floor of the house like never before. For the first time she noticed a photo of Papa's mom and dad. His mom looked exactly as the woman she had met. In a closet was Papa's comic book collection. She thumbed through them and recognized comic books that she had seen in the confectionary store. On the wall in the family room were a number of Papa's guitars on display. He had more guitars than the music store she had visited. *'What a long way he had come from when he was a child.'* She thought.

Little things now had her attention. She noticed nearly two phones in almost every room, and boxes of Kleenex everywhere. Above her head she could feel the cool breeze of the central air conditioning. The one thing that she never had noticed was the huge bookcases and the library of books. There were many books on various historical periods, like the Civil War, plus authors she was familiar with, like Mark Twain and Edgar Allan Poe, and others that she had never heard of, like Rudyard Kipling. There was a whole shelf of almanacs, including one for 1956. She opened one, and since she had never seen an almanac before, she was amazed at the pages and pages loaded with facts. She knew she could spend hours and even days reading these books. She put the 1956 almanac under her arm.

She walked to the door and onto the balcony, where she was greeted by chirping birds and fresh morning air. As she looked out over the beautiful golf course acreage, she heard a train whistle in the distance and instantly a smile came over her face. She hustled down to the kitchen, where her Nana was already stirring things up. "Good morning, baby girl."

"Hi Nana."

Nana grabbed her face by the cheeks. "Let me look at you. Okay, no new wrinkles!" She kidded. "So? How did you sleep?"

"I really had a wonderful dream. It was just so amazing."

"Really, dear? That's wonderful!"

"Where's Papa?"

"Oh, Papa gets up whenever he decides, but never this early. What would you like for breakfast, dear?"

"Can I wait and eat with Papa?"

"It's up to you, sweetie, but if you get hungry just say so. I'll take my coffee and let's go sit and talk."

As Nana poured her coffee, LeeAnn looked around at the kitchen. It was lined with cabinets that had granite tops. The stove alone, with two ovens and a microwave, was impressive. For the first time she noticed the refrigerator was gigantic, with water and ice in the door. She wondered, *'How did they live without a dishwasher or disposal?'* As she stood staring, Nana asked "Are you okay?"

"Sorry Nana, I was just spacing out. Do you think Papa would let me take this book home?"

"Of course! You know how Papa feels about reading; he would be pleased that you had interest in any of his collection. You just take it."

For some strange reason, this question popped into LeeAnn's mind. "Nana, what year was the St. Louis Arch built?"

"That's an easy one. It was built the year that Papa and I met and married, 1967. Why?"

"Oh, it was just something I was curious about. Papa told me he just picked you up and carried you away."

"Well, he might as well have. We knew the moment we met that we would spend our lives together. I don't suppose he told you that I actually had to ask him to dance, did he?"

"No. Really?"

"It is true, but it was not because he was shy, for goodness sake. He did not believe I was over 18, as I looked very, very young. He was a bossy young man and unlike any I had ever met. He was only 20, but he knew the nightclub business as if he had been working in it all his life."

"Did you ever live in Chicago?"

"Yes, when your grandfather was finished with his tour that took us from Florida back to Michigan, we returned to Chicago and rented an apartment there."

"How did you like it?"

"At first, I found it to be overwhelming. Everything from the traffic to the population was hard to adjust to; but after a while, it became interesting and even educational."

"How so?"

"Well, I always wondered how your grandfather could easily identify people by their ethnic origin. He knew Irish and German, Jewish, Polish and Greek by appearance or surname. I found that incredible. It was almost as incredible as his sense of direction. After living in Chicago for a time, I understood how the city was divided ethnically and how great it was learning about other people's cultures and even sampling their foods. I mean, I wasn't stupid, and knew white from black and Hispanics, but Papa knew Italian from Greek and Puerto Rican from Mexican and even Korean from Japanese and Chinese. I had never been exposed to people on an ethnic level, so I enjoyed learning their cultures."

"Papa told me you both had childhoods that were not so great. How bad was yours?"

"Well, my dad died when I was about four and my mom struggled. We lived in south Texas in a small town, and she was a widow woman with a young child. In those days, it was not easy for a woman with a child. We were pretty poor, and eventually she met your great grandpa Walt and we moved to Tulsa. We lived in a little garage house. Initially, times were lean, until my stepfather, your great grandfather Walt, progressed at his career. Those years were not as tough as what your grandfather went through, but it was not your ideal childhood. I experienced fears and deep sadness at the loss of my father, and you know what the anxiety of being introduced to a stepparent can be. I acted out a lot. I had times where I worried about eating, or where we would live, and certainly many times felt self conscious about my clothes, or about our being in poverty. Hearing your mom begging or borrowing can be frightening to a child."

"Did you and Papa really start out with nothing?"

"Absolutely. Your grandfather was making good money as an entertainer, but he was sending most of it home to help his mom. That is something to remember. Always look for a man that treats his mother well, but never a mama's boy. Well, back to the subject. I had nothing and my parents had no faith in what we were doing, so my mom gave us twenty dollars with no card. That is all we had. In their favor, I have to say that meeting a traveling musician and running away with him only after a few days, did seem slightly absurd. Why all the serious questions, young lady?"

"I had this dream…"

"Oh, *that* dream."

"You know about it?"

"Yes, Papa told me what he was going to do."

"How?"

"LeeAnn, I never ask. Your grandfather is difficult to understand, but I learned decades ago not to even try. Just in everyday life, he can baffle me."

"How, Nana?"

"Most people run their lives like a checker game. They see the obvious move and they make it. Your Papa sees life as a chess game. What he does you may not understand until much later. When our daughters would do something that did not seem to be all that bad, Papa might get very upset, because he always knew where whatever they did would take them next. Maybe he sees the future? Honestly, I just learned to accept his instincts, and it has been a wise choice on my part."

"What is the strangest thing he has ever done?"

"I would not even know where to begin. In 1967, we passed through the Ozarks and he predicted this is where we would retire. Twenty years ago when we were still in Illinois, he said we would live next to Andy Williams. Here we are! He always said he would retire in his forties. He did. Sadly, he was burdened and was always concerned about my financial future and I did not understand why? Decades later, he had a near fatal heart attack and I understood that for years he knew it was coming. I now just accept it. He knew the economy would take this downward turn long ago and predicted so many things that are happening today. Some people scoffed at his opinion and many are crying now."

"Is it something he inherited from his family? Will I have this same power?"

"Only you will know that."

"Does he really have O.C.?"

"Oh my goodness, yes; and with a capital C! He has so many symptoms, but he has channeled them well. Look around. Whether its tools, guitars, or guns, he has to have two of almost everything! A few years ago we had two fully furnished homes right down to the tooth brushes! Look in the garage and you will hardly notice that right next to the pop cooler is a second one we use for storage. It took the whole family to get him to give up having two or three cars! I laugh sometimes at his little quirks. Your Papa will give a homeless person ten or twenty dollars without thought, but let a cashier give him the wrong change and he can go berserk over twelve cents! He is really something!"

"Nana, if you could, would you choose to be any younger?"

"Do you mean would I choose to go back in time, or be younger today?"

"Be younger today." LeeAnn quickly replied.

"Absolutely not. The life Papa and I have has just been incredible. What we experienced in technological advances alone is almost unbelievable. My gosh, we saw man land on the moon! **When I was your age,** they put one song on a record that was the size of your head! Now, I'm told the little two inch iPods you have holds hundreds! How can I describe the excitement we experienced with our first color television, or when Papa bought me a microwave oven right after they first came out? They were actually huge, noisy, and cooked terribly, but it was exciting! No, I wouldn't be a day younger."

LeeAnn just smiled as she listened to her Nana.

"It is strange, and young people might never understand, but **when I was you age** we had no area codes or zip codes; no cell phones, fast food, color television, videos, and I could go on endlessly...but life was easier, and we experienced a whirlwind of changes. There was always something new on the horizon. Today, you poor children must be prepared for survival. My goodness, when your mother was born, Papa took me to one of the finest hospitals and the birth of your mother and three day stay was about $750, if my memory is correct. Today, having a child can put one in debt for life!"

It was as if her radar went off, and Nana looked toward the bedroom. "Let me get your Papa some coffee. I can hear him moving about."

LeeAnn had not heard a thing, and really wondered if Nana and Papa had something special beyond normal instincts. She came shuffling back. "He will be out in a minute." She then began preparing breakfast. Everything was already on the counter as she warmed up the stove. It was only a few minutes before Papa entered, and in a mock fashion, asked "Woman, what are you feeding me today?"

"Don't be grumpy with me, or you'll be eating corn flakes!" Nana threatened. "We are having French toast."

Papa gave Nana a hug and sat at the table. "So? How did you sleep, young one?"

LeeAnn wasn't exactly sure how to respond. Did she just have an amazing dream, or was Papa really there on the journey? She hesitated to see if Papa might give her a sign.

"Uh, I slept well." She answered and studied his facial expressions. He made no sign that he knew anything had occurred. For an uncomfortable minute, they sat in silence as Papa sipped his coffee. Then, he turned toward the kitchen and bellowed. "Woman, I am starving! What do I have to do, give you a kick in the caboose?"

Immediately, LeeAnn began laughing, and knew that Papa was there with her and had engineered the whole experience. She watched him sip his coffee with an expression that seemed like nothing special had even happened. "So, can we talk about it?" she requested.

"Didn't I say we would talk a lot?" He smiled.

"Papa, I don't know where to start."

"Best to start at the beginning."

"Do you have any old photographs?"

"I do. I don't have many, but I have some you might enjoy looking at."

Nana set a platter of French toast on the table and a side dish of sausage. As she did, she waved her finger at Papa. "You only get two!" She warned. LeeAnn laughed and her Nana explained. "It takes work to keep this old man from killing himself. He will have to eat cereal for three days to make up for this breakfast. I try to keep him on a heart-healthy diet when I can."

They sat eating quietly until LeeAnn broke the silence. "Nana, did you always cook this good?"

"No, baby girl, I learned the hard way. When I was young, in the Southwest, we learned only one real type of cooking--and that was fried. When I met your Papa--other than eggs and hamburgers--everything he was used to was roasted or boiled in some way. So it took years to blend the two styles and come to a compromise we could both live with. It's one of the two C's of a good marriage. Compromise and Communication are keys to any good relationship."

"Why do so many parents get divorced? If they love each other enough to get married, what goes wrong?"

Both Nana and Papa traded looks and in just a glance, Nana knew Papa had shifted the answer to being her responsibility.

"Well, sweetie, it's like this. It's complicated. Unless two people have the same goals, that alone can create big problems down the line. You're a little too young to be worrying about that."

LeeAnn became serious. "No, I wonder about my mom and dad. What made them not get along after so many years?"

Papa took over for Nana. "Sometimes people realize that they want different things out of life. I won't discuss your parents, because it wouldn't be right, so I'll speak generally. Nana and I had many arguments throughout our marriage. I used to be what is called a 'workaholic'. Working and earning a living was my top priority. I saw that as being correct, because in the end, my motivation was to provide for my family. However, there were times when I missed birthdays or holidays, and I was dead wrong in doing so. The great thing is, that regardless of our arguments, we always came to a compromise. We always had a strict rule that we never call names. That alone starts a cycle where someone calls the other a 'this,' and then the other person calls them a 'that.' The next thing you know they are trying to one-up each other and saying cruel things they can never take back. No name calling was always a strict rule in our house."

Papa continued. "Divorce is not always a bad thing. My mom would not get a divorce, because the church did not allow it, so she would only go through separations, which resulted in reconciliations. Each time my parents got back together, my father--who had a terrible drinking problem which eventually killed him--always became more violent. Had they gotten a divorce, maybe my mom would have had a better life, and possibly my father would have gotten help. Who knows? At your age, it is not something you should worry about. As you can see with Nana and I, regardless of your parental situations or childhood, it will not define your future."

Nana smiled. "You are so serious, young lady. **When I was your age,** I was only concerned with my dolls! Are you concerned about boys?"

"Well, a little."

Papa laughed. "You kids are way ahead of where we were at your age. I admit at ten I found a few girls attractive, and Annette on the Mickey Mouse Club was really something, but girls were not a concern." Papa replied.

Nana also laughed. "We were just not exposed to relationships like you are today. You have all these programs that show young relationships as being 'normal.' That has to put a kind of pressure on you. You dress so well; I already can see you are fashion conscious, and **when we were your age,** fashion was not thought of. We were happy just having clean clothes."

"Let me get some of my old photo albums."

As Papa left to search out the old photo albums, Nana took it as an opportunity to see how the 'dream' affected LeeAnn. "Let me ask you, how did you sleep?"

"Nana, it was like I was gone for days. The whole world was so different. Not at all like today."

"Well you are right about that. We certainly didn't have all the things that you have to worry about. There was no such thing as crimes against children. We never worried about predators or kidnappers or anything like that. We never ever heard any bad language on TV. All in all, we were free to be children and had none of today's stress."

"Nana, when did you first use makeup?"

"I have two answers. Officially, and with parental approval, I was 16 or so, but I would sneak and use some powder and a little lipstick around 15. However, I could never use eye shadow and my lipstick had to be pale pink. Other than that, just a little powder and mascara. Of course, we didn't have the product choices you have today. One thing you should understand, is that parents never want to see their children grow up. Some of it is selfish, but much of it is fear. The longer a parent can keep their child in childhood, the less they have to worry about all the problems adolescence and adulthood will bring. Let me ask…did you learn anything from your journey?"

LeeAnn thought a moment. "Yes, yes I did. I learned a lot. It seemed that I could easily live without texting or my cell phone. I also learned that as I watched Papa, he seemed so independent. He didn't seem to rely on anyone, so I could easily imagine how he was as a young man. I would like to be that independent. It was amazing how many things I did without, and yet I really never missed them. I was also lot less self-conscious."

"How so?" Nana wondered.

"Well, it's not that I didn't care, but how I dressed was just not as important. Nana, they had no designer clothes!"

"I know, baby girl, I was there."

"Nana, nobody locked their doors in the daytime."

"Yes, I know. Screen doors were always open. Nobody had a care in the world, as far as any stranger coming it."

"Nana, what went wrong?"

"I couldn't even begin to explain, and at your young age, you might not fully understand, but we became greedy as a nation. Pretty soon, people wanted bigger houses, bigger cars, more money and the quest for material things literally tore families apart. Families that once lived close to each other began moving to different towns and cities and soon it became a problem to have a simple family get-together. Over the years, families just drifted apart."

"Is that what changed everything?"

"No, not on its own. We also destroyed any respect for authority. The people we looked to for examples began failing us. It didn't matter whether it was the President, or police, or mayor, or priests, or school teachers; corruption became common. Even parents began failing their children. Children became 'latch key' kids, because both parents had to work. In 1956, a person would have had a tough time even finding drugs; in fact, many of today's illegal drugs did not even exist. Today, your Papa and I worry knowing that you will be exposed to drugs in middle school."

Papa returned with a pile of photo albums that he set on the table. He turned to a specific page and asked "Does he look familiar?"

"Yeah, it's you! In fact, you were wearing the same shirt! You were so skinny." LeeAnn giggled.

LeeAnn began looking through the pages. "Look! Here is Butch! Papa, that is your grandparent's house!"

As LeeAnn immersed herself in the old photos, Nana and Papa went about their day with Nana cleaning the kitchen and Papa taking his shower. Every so often, LeeAnn would exclaim "I saw that!" or "I was there!" Eventually, Papa returned and sat with her.

"Papa, why did you take me on that journey?"

"There are lots of reasons. Nana and I could tell you are 10 going on 17. We pretty much know what is going through your young head. I could not give you all the answers you might be searching for, but I knew I could give you a few. Just don't use the bad examples. I mean, if you tried to jump a train today, you would be shot as a terrorist. I wanted you to see that although my life started out pretty rough, obviously it didn't matter to my future. Also, although my mom and dad were not the best parents, it did not matter to the relationships that I created in my life. I remember being your age, and how hopeless I felt. I didn't see any future, and only hoped to make it through each day. When I did think about the future, I became depressed, as I assumed I was predestined to lead a poor and troubled life. None of which was true."

LeeAnn nodded affirmative.

"LeeAnn, all you must do is make yourself as intelligent and strong as you can be, so when the day comes and you step out into the world, you are prepared to climb that building, or jump that train, or do whatever you like to build a great life."

"Papa, how long did you stay away in the children's home?"

"About four years. I was about to be 14, after graduating eighth grade."

"Was everything still the same?"

"No; in 1960, things were much different and continued changing rapidly."

"How did you feel about that?"

Papa smiled. "LeeAnn, I likely felt much like you feel today. My mom and dad were finally divorced and I was still considered a child, so I was unhappy about the situation and the fact that at my age there was nothing much I could do about it. My father died soon after and life was pretty tough."

"Tougher than when you were 10?"

"Yeah, but I was older and stronger and smarter and every year things got a bit better, which is exactly how it will go for you. You will grow into a beautiful, intelligent woman, and everything that may trouble you today will be nothing more than a distant memory."

"Papa, you make me feel much better."

"I hope so, little girl. In the future, I believe Nana will be the one you may want to talk with. She had a tough adolescence and faced a myriad of problems, but she survived."

"Can I talk about any of this?"

"I wouldn't. For one thing, no one would believe you, but also your sister and cousins will most likely take the journey with me in the future as well."

"Can I do it again next year?"

"Unfortunately not, because I can only take you to exactly where I was at that your age and at age eleven, I was in a boy's institution. I just hope you feel a little better about your situation at your age, and remember a world that maybe your generation can recapture."

Nana came in and sat with them and saw the sad expression on LeeAnn's face. She already knew why. "LeeAnn, just because Papa can't do it again, does mean that I can't."

"Really?"

Nana just reached out and took her hand. "Baby girl, just know I will wait until the time is right."

LeeAnn broke into a beaming smile. It was then the doorbell rang. In rushed her sister and cousins. "LeeAnn, dad says we're going to Chucky Cheese tonight!" Ashlee screamed.

"Chill!" LeeAnn replied.

"Chill? Chill? Me no understand!" Papa grunted with a grin.

They all laughed, but only LeeAnn knew the true meaning.

"**When I was your age,** we had no Chucky Cheese." Papa stated.

"Was pizza invented yet?" Krystal joked.

"Yeah, but they were square." Papa answered.

Ashlee began laughing. "Square pizzas? That's funny, Papa!"

"Funny? Then tell me why a pizza is round but they put in a square box? **When I was your age,** pizzas were square and instead of calling them pizza pies, we called them pizza cake! Except that sounded too much like a piece of cake so people all over the world were getting angry when they ordered pizza cake and instead got a piece of cake. So they started making them round so they could call them pies!" Papa explained with his best serious expression. Everyone but LeeAnn was scratching their heads contemplating what sounded logical, but she just laughed.

"Papa, you are hysterical." She replied. She was now looking at her sixty-five year old grandfather, yet also seeing a ten year old jokester.

"Did you eat a lot of pizza when you were our age?" Krystal asked.

"No, not really. **When I was your age** I loved hot dogs and fries with a cold Pepsi! That was my favorite."

"Hot dogs? Nah!" Ashlee replied.

"It's true!" LeeAnn quickly replied.

"How would you know?" Krystal questioned.

LeeAnn looked toward Papa and smiled. "I just do."

"My second favorite is a good, thin crust Chicago pizza. I can eat the whole thing. **When I was your age,** I didn't even let them slice it. I would fold it up and eat it like a giant taco!"

All the girls began laughing. "Was it a pizza taco?" Ashlee asked.

Nana added. "Your Papa can eat pizza right out of the oven. I don't know how he does it? He never burns his mouth. I have no doubt he could fold it up like a taco!"

"How do you do that Papa?" Krystal asked.

"I practiced."

"Why would you practice that?" LeeAnn wondered, expecting a comical answer.

"Well, when I was a teenager, I hung around with a group of guys. We would often pool our money and split a pizza. There was this one guy we called fat Tony, and when they would bring the pizza fresh out of the oven, he would start eating immediately. Well, by the time it cooled down to where everyone else could eat some, fat Tony already had eaten half of the darned thing. So, I practiced until I could eat pizza with fat Tony and get my fair share!"

"Is that true about Papa?" Ashlee asked Nana.

"It is true, sweetie, because I have seen him do it. What I can never understand is why he will whine about his soup being too hot when I serve it, but he can eat a scalding hot pizza. Sometimes your Papa makes no sense!"

"I make no sense?" Papa was ready to respond.

"Don't you say a word or I will hurt you!" Nana threatened, which sent the girls into laughter.

Their laughter was interrupted by the sound of a car horn. "Come girls; help LeeAnn with her things. Your father is waiting."

As LeeAnn went to get her bags, little Madeline, Ashlee, and Krystal gave their Nana and Papa hugs and kisses. LeeAnn was last. She told them "This was the most amazing weekend of my life." Then, they all rushed out and piled into their dad's van and were gone.

"Did you think we did any good?" Papa wondered.

"Time will tell, but I think we did. LeeAnn is far too perceptive for her age. She is already trying to put things together in her little mind that are far beyond her years. I think seeing how you started and knowing who you are now, will help her a great deal. I was a bit younger, but when I realized

I was moving away from what I knew was 'home' and then also getting a stepfather, I really went through some stress and acted out a great deal. Maybe it will stop her from creating her own problems, like I did. Soon, it will be my turn to help her make it through adolescence."

In the van, the girls were anxious to hear about LeeAnn's weekend.

"Did Papa tell you any of his stories?" Ashlee asked.

"Yes, he did. He told me a lot about when he was ten years old."

"Was it funny?" Krystal asked.

"Not always. Papa's dad was not like our dads'. He was real mean."

"Like yelling all the time and giving him time-outs?" Ashlee probed.

"No, like he would drink a lot and hit Papa with his belt."

All the girls became very serious. "Poor Papa." Krystal whispered.

"Sometimes, when he lived with his dad, his dad would just leave him alone for days."

"How did Papa eat and get to school?" Ashlee asked.

"Papa would find pop bottles and cash them in for money. You see, **when Papa was our age,** everything came in glass bottles and you could take them to a store and they were worth a nickel apiece." LeeAnn explained.

"A nickel? Big deal!" Krystal scoffed. "What can you buy with a nickel?"

"It was a big deal, because things were so much cheaper. Papa also used to pitch pennies, which is kind of like gambling."

LeeAnn's dad heard what she said and asked. "Papa gambled when he was ten?"

"Well, it's not exactly like gambling, but it is, kind of. You stand about six feet from the crack on a sidewalk, and you toss a penny or a nickel at the line. The one who gets the closest wins all the money. Papa was real good at it." LeeAnn explained.

"How do you really know?" Krystal asked.

"Uh, he showed me. All I can say, is don't play that game with Papa!"

All the way home LeeAnn answered questions about the weekend and told stories that were actually based on her experiences. The girls, and even her dad, marveled at the knowledge she had accumulated about the fifties, never knowing the knowledge was actually firsthand. Krystal was most interested, because her tenth birthday was coming up in a few short months, and it would be her turn to have a birthday weekend with her grandparents.

LeeAnn was close with her cousin Krystal, for they were nearly the same age. Krystal was her 'adopted' cousin, and had experienced an early life of turmoil and abuse fumbling through the foster care system after being taken away from her birth parents that were deemed unfit due to substance abuse. Adopted at age seven, she still had insecurities left by childhood trauma. She worked hard to catch up with her education level, and knew she was accepted and loved as if she was born into the family, yet the memories of the past still haunted her. LeeAnn knew that a trip with Papa would likely heal some of her old wounds. She wanted to tell everyone of her experience, but knew better, for this was to remain a confidence between her and her Nana and Papa.

There was one person she could share her experience with that would believe her and enjoy hearing of it, and that was her friend, Chloe. LeeAnn and Chloe were close and shared their most intimate feelings. So it was the very next day that LeeAnn sat with Chloe and told her story of visiting the past.

"Can your Grandpa do it again?" Chloe wondered.

"He says he can't, because where he takes me depends on my age, and he was in a boy's home at that time."

"What was the big city like?" Chloe wondered.

"It was fun. There were little stores everywhere you went. You know how people treat us when we go shopping, like they pay no attention to us because they know we have no money, or credit cards? Well in the old days it was the opposite. It was like the store owners paid special attention to children, even if they had no money to spend."

"Like, how?"

"Like they thought children were special. I even had a policeman ask me if I was okay. The man who owned the delicatessen even gave me samples to taste of anything I wanted."

"What's a delicatessen?" Chloe asked.

"They used to sell all kinds of sandwich-type lunch meat, salads, and different specialty foods, like smoked fish."

"Smoked fish? What's that?"

"It's a fish that used to smoke!" LeeAnn joked. They both began laughing. "No; it's a fish that is cooked a certain way. I guess people up north like it. You know they had record stores?"

"I think my grandma Joyce has some records. I don't know why, because no one can play them except her."

"Your grandmother's name is Joyce?"

"Yeah, why?"

"Do you know where she is from? Like where she grew up?" LeeAnn had this feeling that this just may be more than just coincidence.

"Grandma Joyce now lives in St. Louis, that is all I know."

"You should ask your grandma where she grew up. She may have some great stories to tell you."

"She only visits a few times a year. We don't talk all that much." Chloe was quiet for a moment, as if thinking about what she had just said. "You know, I should talk to Grandma Joyce more often. You get to see your grandparents more, and maybe that's why you are so close with them."

"Did you ever think of going to stay with her for a few days?" LeeAnn wisely asked.

"No, I never did. I know she loves me, but I feel that old people don't have much interest in kids our age."

"Well I can tell you by my experience, that I have taught my grandparents about a lot of things. My Nana was amazed at how my iPod works. Sometimes, I feel that because they are older, that they feel scared to ask questions because everyone expects them to know it all. I admit, I hear '**when I was your age**' a lot, but they also ask me an awful lot about my life and how I feel about things."

"Why the sudden interest in my grandma Joyce?"

"Well, the one girl I became friends with was named Joyce. She was very nice."

"That would be just spooky!" Chloe gasped. "Are your grandparents like witches or something?"

"No way. Papa wears a cross and he has the oldest bible I have ever seen. He prays way too much to be a witch. And Nana, she spends all her time making prayer beads, and rosaries, so there's no way."

"Then how can he do that?"

"How do you know that your grandma Joyce can't do the same thing?"

"You think all grandparents can do that?"

"I don't really know? All I know is my Papa sensed my moods and feelings and felt that he could help me."

"Well, did he?"

"Absolutely. You know how you look at your parents and wonder if divorce could happen to you? Or how you see other people with nicer houses and things and you feel that you could never have that? Well, I won't feel that way anymore. What my Papa showed me was that everything I see when I go to his house, I can also have if I want. He was very poor and came from a very dysfunctional family. Even his little brother died! It made me really think. I used to go to their house and assume that they always had nice things, when they really started with nothing. Not even a place to live! When I would see my Papa and Nana hug, I never realized how long they have been together or how they were my age once. There are lots of other things, too, but I don't know if I could ever do them."

"Like what?"

"Well, Papa believes that you should only buy what you can pay for. I guess he doesn't believe in credit cards."

"No credit cards? That sounds crazy."

"It does, unless using credit cards is all you have seen, so you don't know any other way."

"What other way would there be?"

"I guess saving the money?" LeeAnn assumed.

"That would take a long time. Who wants to wait forever to get something? That's all my mom ever uses." Chloe replied. "It sucks to be our age. I know I see my mom do things that I know will cause stress later, and I wonder why she is doing them?"

"My Papa says you can learn two things from your parents. You can learn what to do, and you can also learn what not to do, which is just as important."

"God, I wish my parents were still together."

"Yeah, me too. I asked my Papa why my parents got divorced and it was one question he could not answer. In fact, he said that more than half the people we will meet at our age will be from single parent households, or have stepparents."

"I'll never get married." Chloe stated flatly.

"If I could be like my Nana and Papa, I would. They have been married 44 years."

"God, that's older than my mom!"

"I should try and have you meet them. They are funny. My Nana is really short and my Papa is huge, but she always gets her way. My Papa talks tough, but he always caves to Nana. I know they must love each other, but they really seem to like each other and make each other laugh. Nana is always pinching him when he gets loud or bossy. It's hysterical. It's something I will ask them about the next time I see them. I kind of know how they met and I see how they live now, but how did they get there?"

"When will you see them again?"

"Next time will probably in a few months for Krystal's birthday party."

"Can I come?" Chloe asked.

"We can ask your mom."

"I'll ask her. In fact, I'll ask her when I will get to see my grandma Joyce. Now I'm kind of anxious to ask her about her life."

Chapter Seven

It was months later that the whole family gathered for Krystal's birthday. While Krystal, Ashlee and little Madeline hovered around their Nana in the kitchen, who was putting the final touches on the cake, LeeAnn sat with Papa in the family room.

"Papa, are you and Nana rich?"

"No, I would never say that, but we live well."

"How, Papa?"

Papa reached into his pocket and pulled out a dollar bill and handed it to LeeAnn. "Here, tell me what you don't see on this."

LeeAnn was not sure whether this was to be a joke, but she seriously examined the both sides. Finally, she gave up. "What am I looking for?"

"An expiration date."

Now she really looked close as if expecting to find one possibly in small print. "Papa, I don't see one."

"Bingo! There you go. It never expires. You can hold onto it as long as you like and it will still be good as new. Plus, you can put it in the bank and they will pay you to hold on to it. Now, you're not old enough for me to discuss real estate investments, or the stock market, but I know you understand where I'm coming from."

"Yeah, I have $125 dollars in my bank account."

"Why don't you spend it?"

"Because I'm saving for a laptop computer."

"Exactly. You have a choice to buy many things with $125 dollars, but you are saving it for something much bigger that will also be an asset to your education. It is no different than with adults. We can make a lot of money and the choices are many, but unless we focus on exactly what we really want, life can become very difficult."

"Wasn't it difficult when you and Nana first got married and had nothing?"

"Sure it was. I think we did things pretty much the right way. We faced the difficulty early in life. In our early years, we lived well below our means and saved as much as we could. We also bought some investment property, and I pitched a lot of pennies!" He joked.

"I'm sure! Nana says you worked a lot of hours."

"Yes, I did. But remember, when you are young, that is the time to work hard because you have the energy. If you have the right career, you will also have the passion. When I see a young person wasting their young years, what they don't realize is that they are really extending the time they will be working. Every day they waste is actually a retirement day. I have friends that were goofing off when I was working 60 hours a week. Now I goof off and they are still working. Some took fantastic vacations when they were young, now I am on my vacation. You work now, or you work later; there is no keeping from it. So? If you can't get out of it…get into it and get it over with."

"I think I understand."

"Well, does your teacher ever give you projects for extra credit?"

"Sure."

"Given you're an 'A' student, I imagine you take advantage of that."

"Sure Papa, all the time."

"Life is no different. When I was young, I worked my normal job, and also held a part-time job. That is like extra credit, if you are responsible with your earnings. It's no different. Plus, for a number of years, your Nana also worked. I found it ironic, that when your Nana was working, most women didn't work and she was looked down on a bit. Then, by the time she decided she would no longer work, most women began working."

"I think all women have to work today."

"That's because it's a different world."

"Will Krystal have the dream, Papa?"

"Yes, I think she is ready."

"Can I give you a suggestion?"

"Sure little girl. What would that be?"

"Somehow show Krystal your old photos, so when she sees you, she will recognize you and not be so shocked like I was."

"You know, that's a great idea."

The rest of the girls entered the room. "You should see the cake Nana made!" Ashlee exclaimed.

"Is there enough for me?" Papa asked jokingly.

Krystal decided to tease him. "Nana said you only get a piece this big." She held her finger up to the size of a barely a sliver.

"When I was your age, they didn't even invent birthdays yet!" Papa scoffed mockingly.

"Then how did anyone know how old they were?" Ashlee asked, wisely.

"Nobody knew? We had old geezers going to school and toddlers were drinking beer, and it was a mess! Then, someone said 'let's have birthdays and keep track', and it solved the whole problem."

Even little Madeline laughed, as she already had Papa's number when it came to tall tales.

"Oh, you think that's funny? **When I was your age,** we never sang 'Happy Birthday.' Instead, we sang *'Now you're getting older, soon you're going to keel over!"*

They all laughed hysterically, and leave it to Ashlee to look at Krystal and begin singing "Krystal's getting older, soon she's going to keel over!"

Krystal looked toward Papa. "Look at Papa! He hasn't keeled over yet!"

No sooner than she said it, Papa started leaning and pretended to collapse on the sofa. This brought more laughter. Madeline yelled "Nana, Papa keeled over!"

Nana yelled back. "Just kick him in the butt and he'll be as good as new!"

Immediately little Madeline jumped on the sofa and gave Papa a good kick in the butt, which made him sit right up. They all shared a good laugh.

LeeAnn looked to Papa and asked "Can you show us some old photos?" Before Papa could even answer, she pulled the old albums from a desk drawer and set them in front of him on the coffee table. He looked at her and smiled knowingly, for he knew that LeeAnn wanted Krystal to get a preview of what was to come. The girls gathered around him, with Madeline jumping in his lap.

"Here is one where I was about 10 years old." Papa explained.

The girls all began laughing. "Papa you are so small and skinny!"

"Yeah, I was." Papa made sure Krystal had a good look. Krystal's mom, Papa's daughter, entered the room and immediately asked "Is Papa telling stories again?"

"No, Mom." Krystal answered. "He is just showing us some old pictures."

"Well, did he tell you how he ate at the first McDonald's?"

"No! Tell us Papa!"

"Well, the first one was built in Des Plaines, Illinois, and yes, I ate there when it first opened. In fact, soon after it was built, another franchise opened that, for years, competed with McDonald's. It was called Henry's. It was great, because they competed with each other and their menus were identical, so the prices stayed low for years."

"What happened to Henry's, Papa?" Ashlee asked.

"Well, both started in the late fifties, and Henry's went out of business maybe 15 years later. Then, it became a battle between McDonald's and Burger King."

"You really ate there, Papa?" Krystal asked.

"Yeah, and as I recall, I was able to get a hamburger and a shake for twenty-five cents!"

"Twenty-five cents?" Ashlee gasped.

"Yes; there was a day when a quarter could get you a lot."

"Are you telling stories?" Ashlee challenged.

"No, it really was like that!" LeeAnn interjected.

"How would you know?" Ashlee snapped back.

"Uh, I just do. Papa would never lie."

"**When I was your age,** money meant a lot more. When I think of all the things I could get for a quarter, it does sound kind of like a fantasy. Some day, when you are older and feel like getting depressed, I will explain what inflation is; and boy, we had a bad case of it."

Nana entered the room and added to the wonder of the old days. "What was our first rent for our little apartment…sixty dollars a month?"

"Something like that, but there was a bad side, and that was technological items cost a small fortune. Our first color television had a 21 inch screen and cost me well over $400--but then again, a brand new car was only $3000 dollars."

Papa could see Krystal thinking about what he had said. She seemed to be deep in thought. "What's on your mind, Krystal?"

"Papa, if a car cost only three thousand dollars, how much did a house cost?"

"Well, much like today, there were different priced houses, but you could get a small one for under ten thousand."

"Oh my Gosh!" Krystal responded.

"**When I was your age,** they were even cheaper. You could get a house for four of five thousand, easy."

"Boy, I wish I could have seen that. It seems all everyone cares about today is money."

"Well, sweetie, just make that your birthday wish!"

LeeAnn smiled knowingly.

"Really, Papa?" Krystal asked.

"Sometimes wishes do come true."

It was then that Nana called everyone to dinner. Papa always enjoyed these moments, as the whole family sat together and shared their adventures and concerns. As Nana brought the food to the table, talk centered on Krystal's birthday and her accomplishments at school. Krystal was very proud. Krystal's mom was also very proud. "Krystal worked very hard and made the low honor roll. I hate to say this, but **when I was her age,** at least we had textbooks of our own. Today, all they have is workbooks."

They each shared their concerns for the younger generation. Papa's youngest son-in-law was a police officer, and when he talked, everyone listened with interest. "You would be surprised at how many children are home schooled. So many, that when they are out and about during the daytime, truancy never comes to mind."

"That is quite a change. **When I was their age,** if we skipped school, besides dodging the police, there actually was a truant officer who came looking for you." Papa recalled.

Soon dinner was over, and Nana's birthday cake sat in the center of the table. Just as the candles were lit, leave it to Ashlee to belt out once more, "Krystal's getting older, soon she's going to keel over!"

"What the heck was that?" Nana asked

"Papa said that was the old birthday song!" she replied.

"Well, I am going to have a good talk with Papa!"

"Uh-oh!" Madeline whispered. "Papa is in trouble."

As everyone sang Happy Birthday, Krystal inhaled as deep as she could and when done, she blew out all the candles and made her birthday wish. Afterward, she felt a bit light headed, but felt it was due to holding her breath. Little did she know where she was about to visit. LeeAnn looked at Papa and smiled, as she knew that after this weekend, she and Krystal would have a lot to share and talk about. After all the gifts were opened and the party was nearing an end, Nana and Papa sat with the granddaughters in their living room.

"Now this is Krystal's weekend, but we'll have all of you over for a weekend soon." Nana assured them. It was all hugs and kisses, and soon it was just Krystal, Papa, and Nana sitting alone, as all the goodbyes had been said.

"So, my sweetheart, was it a good party?" Nana asked.

"It was wonderful, Nana."

"It's been a long day, little lady."

Krystal yawned. "Nana, can I get chocolate chip pancakes tomorrow?"

"Sure, this is your weekend. You can have whatever you like; but for now, you should get a good night's rest."

Krystal gathered her things and gave Nana and Papa a kiss and proceeded to bed. She loved sleeping over, and being alone, she had the whole guest room and king size bed to herself. She stretched out across the middle and soon she was fast asleep. She felt strange, because she 'awoke' with her foot dangling off the bed. '*Weird! I must be sleeping on the edge?*'

She opened her eyes, and much like LeeAnn had been shocked, so was she; because instead of the king size bed of Nana and Papa's, she was in a small twin bed in a room that was totally unfamiliar. For an instant, she had flashbacks of her years being fostered and shuffled back and forth between strange homes. "MOM!" she yelled.

As she looked around at what to her seemed like old fashioned furniture, it was a double shock when her mom entered wearing some kind of floral house dress. "Get up young lady; I have to get the store opened."

"The store?"

"Yes! Your father is there alone and he can't fix appliances and wait on customers at the same time. I left some cereal on the table. Just be sure to be home for supper, and please, if the phone rings and you're here, take a message."

"Why? Does the voice mail not work?"

Krystal's mom looked at her strangely and asked "Voice mail? What in the world are you talking about? You are the voice mail."

Krystal glanced at the huge black telephone with a pad and pencil next to it, and began to realize this must be a dream. '*What is this? Where am I?*' She wondered. Her observances were much the same as LeeAnn's, as she examined her closet and then proceeded to the bathroom. As she washed and then went to choose her outfit for the day, her mind was spinning. '*What did mom mean? Be home by dinner? Does this mean I can just go out?*'

She walked through the house completely forgetting about breakfast, and felt as if she was in a museum. When she entered the living room, besides being astonished by the tiny television screen, she could see through the front window a boy about her age. She was in a small bungalow house with a huge picture window, and out on the front sidewalk was a boy that looked like the photo she had seen of Papa. *'No way!'* Krystal opened the front door and asked meekly. "Papa?"

"Hi, Krystal. Come on, let's have some fun!"

"I can just leave?"

"Sure! Welcome to 1956."

Krystal followed along and much like LeeAnn entered a world that would continue to amaze her. She followed a similar adventure as LeeAnn and marveled at the elevated train and electric buses. It was hard to imagine this world of nickel pop and penny candy ever existed. It was on the second day that Krystal and Papa sat on stainless steel vents and looked out over the city from the top of Papa's pigeon factory, after climbing the old fire escape to the roof.

"Papa, why did you do this? How did you do this?" Krystal asked.

"I thought this would help you."

"Well I feel luckier than you. You have to go to an orphanage next month."

"Don't feel bad, as it all comes out okay for Papa in the end as you well know."

"Didn't you feel lonely and scared?"

"I was used to being alone, and it was not as scary as one might think. It certainly was not as scary as you going to strange homes in the foster system."

"I was scared a lot."

"Well, I knew what you were feeling and the insecurities you might face in having been adopted."

"I sometimes become insecure, as I fear it could all end."

"No, it will never end. Let me tell you this; whether you are related or not, really may or may not mean anything throughout your whole life. No one treated me worse than my own father! Remember this; only pay 5% of your attention to what people say, and 95% of your attention to what they do. Whether you are related or not is just not a factor. There will be people that will tell you they love you, and will not be there when you need them. Most important, is that there will be people in your life that may not say much, or be able to say 'I love you,' yet they will always be there for you. Always watch what people do, never what they say."

"I think I understand."

"I hope so, because you are about to enter an age where you may want to test your parent's love for you. Likely you might decide to push their limits. Know this; that they will take everything you can throw at them, and they will always love you. I know what you are thinking and that is; will they ever send me away? The answer is no. They will stand by you and never stop loving you. You are surrounded by people that love you dearly, even though a few may not say so, just watch their actions and that will speak volumes. Always recognize when a person just does something kind, because that action is far more valuable than words."

"I think I understand."

"Look at me. See my filthy jeans? No one cares to wash them, or iron them, or fold them up for me. I will go home tonight and wash these by hand in the sink. What do you see in your closet? That is love. I don't care whether it was cereal, or eggs for breakfast, that was a bit of love. Remember that. When your parents push you to do homework, that is love. If they didn't love you, they would not care whether you learn anything or not. Do you think anyone cares if I do my homework? In fact, my father couldn't care less if I even come home tonight. You will soon be in your teens, and all kinds of people will be talking at you. Remember to only listen to those who really care."

"I'll try."

"I worry about all you girls. Words have become near meaningless. People say 'I love you' like they say 'hi' or 'bye.' Watching people's actions and being able to recognize people who have your best interest at heart will be very important as you grow."

As Krystal contemplated Papa's words, a faint train whistle could be heard in the distance. "Papa, the train is coming! You said we would ride."

"Come on, we have got about ten minutes. Let's go!"

There was nothing that Krystal missed out on, as her journey was only slightly different than LeeAnn's. She also found that she could do without all the gadgets that dominated life in 2011. She had the same sadness when she awoke and her visit to the past was over. As she sat on the king size bed, she stared at her cell phone, and didn't have the usual compulsion to begin texting. Instead, she looked forward to Nana's chocolate chip pancakes and talking with her grandparents. She found herself looking at her open suitcase and all the clothes folded neatly. *'Mom did that.'* She thought, remembering Papa's words and how he had to wash his jeans in the sink. She took a clean pair of jeans out of the suitcase and when she did, a note fell out that had been folded in with them.

Dear Krystal,
Have a great weekend with Nana and Papa.
Miss You! Love You!

Mom

Her Eyes welled up with tears as she knew she was surely loved. She quickly prepared for breakfast with two more people that loved her dearly.

"Good morning baby girl!"

"Hi Nana."

"Are you ready for your pancakes?"

"Is Papa up yet?"

"I just took him his coffee, and I'm sure he'll be out in a minute."

"Nana, did you have it as tough as Papa when you were a child?"

"No, but my childhood was different. After my dad died, my mom saw a few men. I could always sense that they liked my mom, but didn't want me. It is a horrible feeling when you know you are not wanted, but that isn't anything you should be thinking about."

"Papa and I talked a bit about that."

"I think he may have been telling you to look around and be thankful and appreciate what you have, and never, ever, take it for granted."

"Nana, sometimes I'm just afraid that it will all go away."

"Happiness is like that. Don't think Papa and I don't hold our breath and thank God every single day. From our modest beginnings, look at us! We have wonderful children and son-in-laws, beautiful, intelligent granddaughters, good health and a very nice roof over our heads. Now, add to that some crispy bacon and chocolate chip pancakes!"

"I guess you're right Nana."

"No, I know I'm right. You will find that there are many people that cannot deal with true happiness. Happiness is not just laughing all the time like a fool. Happiness is being secure; being surrounded by loved ones. Happiness is feeling well, and not being hungry. Some people refuse to be happy in a true sense. They chase a feeling that is always fleeting and can never be sustained, therefore they are always unfulfilled. I hope someday you will understand how happy it makes me to see your smile when I pile those pancakes on your plate! So many people don't realize that happiness is simply not being unhappy! Let me ask you; are you happy right now?"

"Yeah, Nana."

"Why?"

"Well, I am with you and Papa and I'm having my favorite breakfast, and I feel good inside!"

"Remember this feeling! Presents are nice, laughing is fun, but this feeling is the best in the world."

Out of nowhere, Papa entered, bellowing "The best feeling is my plate full of food, woman!" He looked to Krystal and smiled. "Good morning, my beautiful freckle-faced granddaughter!"

"Good morning Papa!"

Their discussion took most of the morning and soon, the doorbell rang and the special weekend was over. Krystal left with a whole new perspective and a whole new bond with her grandparents. She also held a secret that she could only share with LeeAnn. As time passed, no one understood the special bond between LeeAnn, Krystal and their Grandparents. Family gatherings always held a special moment, when maybe a 'key' word was mentioned that triggered glances between them, like whenever Papa used the word 'caboose'. The few years seemed to flash by, as all too soon it was Ashlee's tenth birthday.

That evening was much like any other birthday weekend, except LeeAnn and Krystal knew what Ashlee was in for. Because her birthday was in April, it would be that month of 1956 she was about to visit. As always, the girls gathered in the living room with Papa. He looked over them with great pride. LeeAnn and Krystal, at age 12, looked very much like young ladies. Little Madeline was now no longer the baby, and enjoying the mischievous age of six. While the older girls now had more serious questions, little Madeline was the one bringing humor to the get-togethers.

"Papa, why is your hair getting so white?" Madeline asked innocently.

"That's a good question Maddy, but the real puzzle is why the hair is falling out on top of my head, and instead growing out of my ears!"

Maddy became serious. "Really? You have hair growing out of your ears?"

"Yeah, Nana has to trim my ears just like the dogs!" Papa joked.

"Nana! Is Papa telling stories?"

"What baby girl?" Nana asked.

"Do you trim Papa's ears?"

"I sure do! I also have to trim his eyebrows which grow like weeds."

Madeline climbed up next to Papa and began inspecting his ears. This brought laughter to the other girls.

"What have you got there?" Papa asked looking at her little wrist watch.

"Mom bought me this watch." Madeline quickly answered.

"**When I was your age,** we didn't have watches like that. In fact, most times we never cared what time it was."

"How did you know when to have lunch?" Madeline asked smartly.

"**When I was your age,** we just ate when we were hungry. Who said that you had to eat lunch at 12 o'clock?" Papa asked in jest.

"Mom." Madeline quickly replied.

"Well, your mom is never wrong. So you'll do well paying attention."

"I listen, or I get a time out." Madeline answered seriously.

Papa smiled and everyone knew a whopper was coming on. "See? **When I was your age,** we had no time outs, because no one knew what time it was."

"Really?" As the other girls laughed, Madeline was curious. "If there were no time outs, what did they do to punish you?"

"Oh, we got spanked but good!" Papa replied.

As the girls laughed, little Madeline serious stated "I'll take the time outs!"

"Girls, we're about ready for the cake and to sing Happy Birthday." Nana announced.

Papa's old joke of a song had stuck with them, and Madeline began singing, "Ashlee's getting older, soon she's going to keel over!"

"No keeling over today!" Papa announced.

"Papa, I wish I had a dollar for every time you say **when I was your age!**" Ashlee wisely stated. "I wish I could see if all you say is really true."

"Well, make that your birthday wish! You never know what can happen."

This statement brought serious glances between LeeAnn and Krystal, because they knew that Ashlee had said the magic words. As they finished singing Happy Birthday, Ashlee easily blew out the 10 candles. Ashlee was happy, as being 10 was a big deal in her mind. It was two digits, and a step toward her teens. Papa was always amazed at how mature the girls were by age ten. They still loved their toys, but yet seemed to have adult perspectives on so many current affairs. This always brought a hint of sadness to him, because it seemed children never had the enjoyment of a pure childhood. Never were they to enjoy a day without some fear or concern of some kind. Just thinking of the current news made Papa fearful. It was normal for schools to be locked down because of threats. Shootings at schools had become all too common. Drug sweeps through schools by local police began in middle school. So Papa looked forward to showing Ashlee a day without care or concern.

After the gifts had been opened and the family had said their goodbyes, Ashlee sat with Nana and Papa, tired from a long day of fun. Papa lifted her head and gave her a serious look. "Nope! No new wrinkles yet."

"Papa, no one gets wrinkles at 10!" She laughed.

"Oh yes they do! There is a real disease that ages children so by the time they are 10, they look like they are 80!"

"Nana, is that true?"

"Unfortunately, baby girl, yes. Your Papa is telling the truth, but you have no worries, because it shows up at infancy. Papa and I would like you to stay 10 for a long time, because childhood is so fleeting. You girls are growing up much too fast."

"Papa, do you remember when you were 10?"

Papa reached for his picture album. "Here sweetie, this is what I looked like at ten. I was actually small and skinny for my age."

"Wow! You were little."

"Then I discovered little sugar donuts and look what happened!"

"Nana, is that true?"

"No baby girl, your Papa is telling a whopper."

Ashlee yawned, and they knew it was time for her to retire to her journey.

"I think it is bedtime, baby girl."

"Will you tell me a story, Papa?" she asked.

"Not tonight, sweetie. I don't think you will be awake long enough."

Ashlee gathered her things and kissed her grandparents good night and proceeded to the guest bedroom with a welcoming king size bed. With her head on the pile of soft pillows, and covered in the fluffy down quilt, she was asleep in minutes.

She was shocked when she awoke to her mom shaking her. Not realizing where she was, she asked "Mom, what are you doing here?"

"Wake up young lady. I'm supposed to be here."

Ashlee was confused, as she looked around at the 'old' furniture and her mom who appeared in some old fashioned costume.

"Mom, what's going on?"

"What's going on is that I'm leaving for work, and you should get ready for school!"

Ashlee's birthday was in April, so in 1956, school was in full gear. She was in the same apartment that LeeAnn had also visited. Ashlee was very particular about her clothes, so it was in horror when she opened the closet. '*What the heck is this?*' She saw no traces of her stuff, and the clothes in the closet appeared ridiculous. She spotted the school uniform dresses immediately. *'Oh my God. I am expected to wear this?'*

Much the same as LeeAnn and Krystal, she was amazed as she looked about the old fashioned kitchen and made her way to the bathroom. *'This must be some kind of weird dream.'* After washing up and fixing her hair, she donned the school dress and ate the bowl of cereal her mom had left for her. It was only after she looked out the kitchen window did she realize she was in a second floor apartment. On a chair were her books and a silly children's lunch box. *'Okay, I'll play along.'* With no trace of her sister, she began to hope she would awake soon. *'Look at the size of that phone! That's hilarious."* She skipped out the front door and down the stairs and as she stepped out into the sidewalk, she froze in shock; for there was the skinny little boy from the picture Papa had shown her. "Papa?" She asked.

"Hi, Ashlee. Are you ready for an adventure?"

"How?"

"Don't ask; it's magic!"

"This is LeeAnn's and Krystal's secret, isn't it?"

"Yes, they have both been here."

Off they went, following a similar routine. Ashlee had a full day of Catholic school, which really made her understand Papa's dissatisfaction with the school system of 2012. Just the number of books she had been given was surprising. After school, like LeeAnn, she found the Mickey Mouse Club mesmerizing and totally enjoyable, even on the tiny black and white TV screen. As the adventurous journey continued, the elevated train and electric buses were fun, and the shops really did remind her of Disneyworld's Main Street. She was amazed at the endless miles of little neighborhood shops and people hustling about. Much like LeeAnn, she was happy, yet sad to be with her mother and father, who in the real world had been divorced for years. Eventually, they climbed the fire escape to the roof of Papa's secret place and looked out over the city. As always, there came the serious questions.

"Why, Papa?" She asked and he knew exactly what she meant.

"Lots of reasons little one. I wanted you to see how things used to be. I also wanted you to realize that the constant communication and media bombardment was unnecessary. I wanted you to sample a world where the word stress was hardly known and to have a chance of walking around without fear. In your case, I wanted you to have a glimpse of how it was when your mom and dad were together. Since you are the first one to accuse me of telling tales, I wanted you to know when I say 'w**hen I was your age**,' most times I'm not kidding."

"I certainly believe you now!"

"I hope this helps you see things a little clearer. I know you hold your feelings in and when you can't any longer, you explode every now and then. You can see how it was with me and know that soon, you will be controlling your own destiny. You are ten now, and you can start to voice your concerns and not hold things in all the time. Believe me, your parents love you and if you talk, they will listen."

"Papa, did you ever have a stepmother or stepfather? "

"No, I never did."

"Then you don't really know how it is."

"You are correct, but I do know this; the people in your life that will love you, may or may not be related to you by blood. If your stepparents are there for you and protect and feed you and make sure you are well cared for, make no mistake, they love you too, whether they can say it or not. Watch their actions. Pay little attention to what people say, but always pay attention to what they do. Sometimes the kindest, most loving people have trouble verbally expressing their feelings, while others are all talk and not much more."

"You have always told us this."

"Well, it's true. Krystal knows I am not her grandfather through blood relation, yet I know that she knows I love her as one of my own. In my mind, it just does not matter. She is my grandchild, as sure as you are. I happen to be lucky in that I have no trouble expressing my feelings, but even if I never told her, she knows I love her dearly through my actions. I will always be there for her and for little Madeline, as I am for you and LeeAnn."

"It's tough Papa. My stepparents act like my parents, but they are not. I have my real parents but they're just not together."

"Imagine how they must feel? Don't you think your stepmom worries if she is living up to your image? Believe me, it's not easy being a stepparent. They fear your rejection. Just let them know you appreciate them and that their efforts will mean everything to them. You should ask Nana, because she had a stepfather after her real father died."

This struck a chord with Ashlee. She realized that she had not really accepted them as well as she could have, and began thinking of all the kind things her stepparents had done in the past. "You're right, Papa."

As they sat in silence and Ashlee contemplated her grandfather's words, the faint sound of the train whistle could be heard in the distance.

"Will we really ride the top of a train Papa?"

"Yes. We certainly will. Are you ready?"

"Yeah! Did LeeAnn and Krystal ride it?"

"Yes, they did. Do you know what a caboose is?"

"Well, the way you use the word with Nana by telling her you will whack her in the caboose; it must mean a butt." She laughed.

"Well, I'll show you what a caboose truly is, and as far as butts, you are about to fall on yours!"

"No Papa!"

"Have you ever had tumbling in gym class?"

"What's tumbling?"

"Never mind."

"No, really!"

"**When I was your age,** we had a gym class called tumbling. It was where they taught you how to fall and jump without hurting yourself."

"Huh?"

"Okay, you will fall on your butt, but it won't be too bad. I promise."

Their adventure continued and Ashlee found that there really was a time when a penny was important. There was a time when children moved about safely and without concern and when everyone seemed a bit kinder. As with LeeAnn and Krystal, she never missed her cell phone or any of the modern gadgets that occupied so much of her modern life. Most of all, she enjoyed the freedom that children were allowed.

All too soon her journey was over and she found herself stretching and waking up in Nana and Papa's king size bed. Ashlee was slightly sad that her trip ended, but excited that she could now share her experience with LeeAnn and Krystal. She hurried and washed and dressed and went down to the kitchen, where Nana was already preparing breakfast.

"Do I get whatever I want for breakfast?"

"Well, good morning to you too!"

"Good morning Nana, I'm sorry."

"Well baby girl, I'm making one of your favorites."

"Which one?"

"Eggs with cheese on top."

"Where's Papa?"

"Oh, he just gets up whenever he feels like it."

"Nana, how did you feel about having a stepfather?"

"I did not like it as a child. I missed my real father and I guess I acted out and made it tough on my stepfather. I think I was an example of how not to act."

"Why?"

"Well, although he cared for me and wanted a good relationship, I always seemed to keep my distance and push him away. In little ways, I always reminded him he was not my real father. I was very troubled."

"I guess I'm troubled at times." Ashlee admitted.

"You must realize that despite what could be considered poor circumstances, you have the best situation. You have two fathers and two mothers, even though some are stepparents."

"I never really thought of it that way."

Papa entered, bellowing as usual. "Whose caboose am I kicking in order to get a plate of eggs? I want eggs!"

Nana pursed her lips. "I'm going put a goose egg on your head in a second. Go sit and drink your coffee."

"So how did you sleep?" Papa asked.

"You know. At least now I understand all the inside jokes, especially the caboose thing."

"I just hope it helps you look forward to the future. All of you girls are so mature for your age and will be faced with so many choices and obstacles, I wanted you see how things could be and that your childhood problems don't have to affect your adult life." Papa said seriously.

"It sure was different Papa. How did you not get depressed? I get depressed at times."

"Oh, I got depressed all the time, but depression is just a part of living. Logically, life will present you with many things to be depressed about. Think about it. Things will break, people you love will get ill or maybe even die. Friends may move away. You will get old like Nana and I, and may have health problems, which are all good reasons to be depressed. What I do, is let depression take its toll for a reasonable period, but then snap out of it and go on."

"Sometimes I'm just not happy."

Papa laughed. "Not happy? Not being happy is fairly normal and a lot different from being unhappy. If you have a day where everything goes right and you feel healthy but just not exuberant, that is not being depressed or unhappy, it is normal. Does that make sense?"

"Kind of."

Ashlee's tone did not sound positive.

"Sweetie, at ten years old, despite your maturity, this is a tough subject, but an important one. When you see people who suffer from addictions, they are chasing what they believe is a happiness of some type. It can be drugs, or even credit cards. People try to continuously chase that 'feel-good' feeling. Those special moments, when you buy something you really wanted, or go to Chucky Cheese, or open Christmas presents are just that; special moments. They are not to become the definition of normal."

"Papa, how do you know if you're happy?"

"Let me ask you; how will you feel in a few minutes when your dad and sister come to get you?"

"Happy…I guess?"

"There you go. Yes, you will feel happy, because you are loved and you love them and miss them. Just being with people you love and who love you is the greatest happiness you can have. Remember that! When you are twenty years old, I will ask you to write down the three moments in your life that made you feel the best. I promise, they will all be special moments of love and security. None will have anything to do with presents or buying stuff or anything money can buy. There is no amount of money that can give Nana and I the happiness of watching you grow into a beautiful young woman."

The doorbell rang and LeeAnn came rushing in. "Hi, Nana. Hi, Papa. Come on Ashlee, dad is waiting." LeeAnn actually was anxious to talk with Ashlee about her trip with Papa. She immediately went to Nana and gave her a big hug.

"What are you doing today?" Papa asked.

"We have a soccer game and dad is coaching."

"Well, you girls have fun."

Soon they were gone and Nana and Papa sat alone.

"God, they grow up so fast." Nana stated sadly.

"Come on, admit it. We are all only ten year olds at heart. Do we ever really grow up? I believe we are all just a bunch of aging ten year olds."

He walked to a shelf and began thumbing through an old vintage comic of Lady and the Tramp, dated 1956.

Chapter Eight

AS THE YEARS PASSED, THE family gathered for LeeAnn's 15th birthday. They were scattered about the house, with Nana in the family room with the older girls, and Papa in his office showing a 9 year old Madeline his old comic books.

"Papa, I can't believe these were 10 cents?"

"Yeah, **when I was your age,** ten cents was a lot of money."

"Today they can cost more than five dollars."

"Yeah, I know. It's really a shame, because children can't afford them any longer. What I get a kick out of, is now that adults are reading them, they are called graphic novels. That's a bunch of crap, because they are all just comic books."

Madeline laughed, for it seemed the older Papa got, the more outspoken and opinionated he became. Her laughter gave Papa warm feeling of pleasure. As they thumbed through the comics, Madeline's phone rang and she looked at the little screen.

"Important?" Papa asked.

"Nah, just Jill sending me a text."

"I'm sure it's something urgent like she just went to the bathroom." Papa joked.

"Papa, it's what we do."

"What else can you do on that thing?"

"I can listen to music or even watch a movie." She boasted.

"Who would want to watch a movie on that little thing? That's why the Asian people have squinty eyes, from looking at all that tiny crap."

Again Madeline laughed. "Papa you're funny!"

Meanwhile in the family room, Nana was holding court of her own. "**When I was your age,** there was no way we could wear our skirts that short."

"I don't know Nana, I saw some photos of you and Papa when you were young and you were pretty hot!" LeeAnn replied.

"I was 19 by then. **When I was your age,** I couldn't even wear make-up."

"You told me you wore make-up." Ashlee quickly responded.

"Yes, but I had to sneak it."

"Did you date?" Krystal asked.

"Date? No way. My parents wouldn't hear of it. In fact, they timed me everywhere I went. The only way I could talk to a boy, was either at school, or on my part-time job as a waitress."

"What was your favorite song back then?"

Nana thought for a second. "I liked anything by the Everly Brothers, or 'Pretty Woman' by Roy Orbison."

"Everly Brothers?" Krystal questioned.

"In Tulsa, we had all kinds of music. We had a lot of country music, some rock and roll, and even some rhythm and blues. The Everly Brothers were probably one of the first cross-over artists. They were country, but it seemed everyone loved their music."

"Papa said you used to dance." Ashlee prodded.

"Yes, I did. In fact, I danced professionally for a short time. That's what I was doing when I met your Papa."

"What kind of dances did you do?" LeeAnn asked.

"Oh, they all had funny names, like the Boogaloo!"

They all laughed and began repeating "Boogaloo? Boogaloo?"

"What's the Boogaloo?" Ashlee asked.

"I wish I could have seen that! Nana doing the Boogaloo!" Krystal immediately began dancing around, causing hysterical laughter.

"I wish I could have seen you at 15." LeeAnn stated.

Hearing the laughter, Papa and Madeline joined the group. Papa knew that for these adolescent years, the girls were no longer his and would become Nana's girls during these formative years. Much like with his daughters, it was Mom that had to guide them through this period of emotional turmoil and physical change. So now, Nana would help them move from young ladies to young women.

"Don't laugh, your Nana used to shake a mean booty!" Papa joked.

"Come on Nana! Shake your booty!" Krystal pleaded.

"Your Nana's booty shaking days are long gone girls." Nana said firmly.

"Were you a good dancer Nana?" LeeAnn asked.

"**When I was your age,** besides school dances which were rather lame, we used to go to a roller rink where they held dances and even had live bands. Ike and Tina Turner used to play there all the time."

"Ike and who? " Ashlee asked.

"They were big back in the day." Papa explained.

Papa sat back and watched his little girls who were now young ladies. Even his little Madeline would be 10 next year and would be going on what would be his last trip back in time. '*Where did time go?*' He wondered as they talked with Nana about boys, dating, fashion, and their futures. It was her turn, as it seemed every other sentence she spoke began with '**when I was your age.**' This was always followed by doubtful or humorous comments.

"Nana, did the boys pick you up for a date on horses?" Ashlee joked.

"No! Even though it was Tulsa, we had cars." She replied. "**When I was your age,** the boys came to door and properly introduced themselves. They also opened the door and always paid for the date."

"It's a lot different today, Nana. We sort of meet at the show or the mall without our parents even knowing." LeeAnn replied.

"Boy, I would kick them in their caboose!" Papa interjected. "We had a rule in our house. No boy could come to the door with hair longer than my daughters and God help them if they had tattoos or any metal in their faces. I would have slammed the door in their face!"

LeeAnn looked at Nana. "Is that true?"

"It sure is. Papa also had another rule and that was if a boy brought a motorcycle to the house, it became his. Never could our girls ride on a motorcycle."

The girls all knew that Nana was not kidding. They knew Papa could roar like a lion when upset and no one wanted to be on the receiving end of his displeasure. "All fathers are strict. A father always wants his daughter to be treated like a princess with respect. The problem today, is that women are always being compared with men on the basis of equality. There is no question that we should be treated equal, but this logic has been distorted to a physical level. There is no question that men and women are so different that they cannot be compared. It is apples and oranges. Today, you girls watch movies or television and it is common to see a woman fighting with a man. This is wrong and unrealistic. These images basically endorse the fact that a man can become physically violent toward a woman. **When I was your age,** a man didn't dare raise his hand to woman. You poor girls have to learn self defense and to guard your drinks from being drugged, not to mention protecting yourself just walking home. It worries the heck out of Papa and me."

"So you never had to worry about going out with a strange boy?" Krystal asked.

"Well, I never really considered going out with a stranger. But to answer your question, no. I never really worried and never had to guard my drinks. It was a different time."

"What about Papa? He was a traveling musician and he was strange?" Ashlee logically asked.

Nana laughed. "Look at him. Look at those eyes. Do you see anything there but kindness?"

"Yeah, but Papa's eyes can change." Ashlee replied.

"And they will, if any of you girls bring a boy here with tattoos or metal in his face!" Papa declared.

Krystal announced. "My mom has tattoos!"

"No she don't!" Papa answered.

"Yes she does, Papa!"

"I said, no she don't, and I don't want to hear otherwise! You girls will have to learn, what Papa doesn't know, Papa can't get upset about. I won't ask, and you don't tell!" He stated firmly.

Krystal excused herself, explaining she had to call her boyfriend.

"**When I was your age,** we wouldn't think of calling a boy. They had to call us."

"It's just to talk Nana." She replied as she rushed off.

Soon, it was time for the family dinner and one of Nana and Papa's favorite moments. Everyone looked forward to Nana's cooking and her homemade birthday cake. As everyone took a seat, Papa surveyed the room and stated "We're going to need a bigger table soon." LeeAnn and Ashlee's dad and stepmom were there, as well as their mom and stepdad, plus Krystal's mom and her husband who was in full police uniform, then add all the girls and there was a house full. When Krystal returned, Papa gave her a stern glance.

"Does he have hair longer than yours?"

Krystal laughed. "No, Papa."

"Then does he have metal in his face?"

Again she laughed. "No, Papa."

Ashlee sat next to Nana, who closely examined her face. "Is that lip gloss?"

"Yes Nana, just a little."

"Boy, **when I was your age,** I couldn't get away with that."

Papa laughed. "They didn't have lip gloss in those days. The girls all used lead paint!"

This brought laughter to the whole table. It was Papa's son-in-law, the policeman, that dominated the conversation with all the humorous stories that he felt appropriate for family conversation. Wisely, many of his recounts had subtle messages for the girls. He never brought the tragedies up, except those that involved teens and situations that could and should have been avoided.

"Did the boys from Forsyth really try to steal the Branson goal posts?" LeeAnn asked.

"Yes, those little idiots never realized how big they were. They got them out of the ground and didn't know what to do after that!" He explained.

"Did you arrest them?" LeeAnn asked.

"Yes, it was vandalism, but they meant no real harm. They won't have a record and will only do some community service, plus having to live it down."

"These kids today are lucky! **When I was their age,** a policeman would have put his boot up my butt! There was no such thing as police brutality back then." Papa responded.

"Yeah, times have changed. We must be pretty careful as to how we respond to people, especially young people." He replied.

When dinner was finished, Nana had no shortage of help in the kitchen, as all the girls were anxious to have cake. Soon, everyone was singing Happy Birthday to LeeAnn. At 15, LeeAnn was at that age where the birthday song made her a bit embarrassed. In one breath, the candles were out and wrapping paper was scattered about as the presents piled up.

"Is this the best birthday ever?" Papa asked.

LeeAnn smiled and winked back. "No, my tenth birthday was the best so far."

Papa just smiled. There is no way to describe the warmth and love of three generations blending in harmony. They all made short work of the cake and soon all the goodbyes were said and it was just Nana, Papa, and LeeAnn alone in the family room.

"Fifteen is a wonderful age, baby girl." Nana stated.

"Next year I can get my driver's license."

"Don't be so anxious to drive. It can be quite dangerous."

"It's not that I want to drive so much, it's that it will give me a little freedom to go out by myself now and then. Aside from school functions, I have to rely on my parents going with me everywhere."

"That is a bit sad, because even though my parents were strict, I was able to go shopping or travel by bus to my grandma's after school or on weekends. Yes, **when I was your age,** there was little concern for my overall safety."

LeeAnn yawned, as she was tired from a long exciting day. "Nana, I wish things were like that now. I always have to be aware of people around me, even at the mall."

"**When I was your age,** I just worried about the boys whistling or making comments. You should get a good night's sleep, baby girl."

Papa just listened and nodded in agreement, as LeeAnn gave them both a hug and climbed the stairs to the familiar guest room. Once she was gone, Papa looked to Nana.

"Is it time?" He asked.

Nana nodded positive. "Yes, it is time."

"She should have fun, as 1961 was a great year."

Nana laughed. "You were 15 in 1961, but I was 15 in 1963!"

"1963 is even better. The Beatles were here and all kinds of cultural changes were taking place."

"The Beatles weren't that big in Tulsa yet until 64. Remember how slow things moved across the country. We were just getting Motown."

"Boy, I wish I could go with you." Papa lamented. "I was just starting to play bass professionally that year."

"You were traveling in a band, and I was still waiting to date! What a difference a few years make when one is young. Ah, let's go to bed. I've got some traveling to do."

LeeAnn had one of the best night's rest ever, which was normal for sleeping at her grandparents. When she awoke, she looked up at the ceiling and it was pink. *'Weird? The ceiling is white?'* She rubbed her eyes and looked again, but it remained pink. She sat up and realized she was in a twin bed, and the whole room was pink. On the nightstand was even a pink lamp. *'What the heck?'* Across the room was a second twin bed, and someone was asleep and covered head to toe. She got up and pulled the covers back, expecting it to be Ashlee. Instead she was shocked, for in the bed was none other than a 15 year old Nana!

"Nana? Is that you?" She whispered.

Nana stretched and yawned and softly said "Good morning baby girl."

"What is happening? What year is this?"
"This is 1963!"
"Why 1963?"
"Because that's when I was your age."
"Where are we?"
"You are on a sleepover at my house. Welcome to Tulsa."
"What are we going to do?
"Let's go have some fun, baby girl!"